Owned by Pirates

haley travis

Romance for unconventional, interesting folks.

Sometimes strong, quirky women need a life shake up, not a man. But these things never go as planned, do they?

Blog: haleytravisromance.blogspot.com
Email List: http://eepurl.com/gd7WDP

Copyright 2020 Haley Travis. All rights reserved.
Cover and Book Design by LexieRenard.com.

No part of this book may be reproduced, stored in a retrieval system, or transmitted or duplicated in any form whatsoever without express written permission of the author.

This book is intended for sale to adults only. This is a work of fiction. Any similarities to actual people or specific locations is completely coincidental, or intended fictitiously. All characters are over 19, no sex partners are related, all sex is consensual. This is fantasy. In the real world, everyone practices safe sex at all times. Right? Right.

Owned by
Pirates
haley travis

***

TABLE OF CONTENTS

***

~ Prologue ~ Flora ~

* The Night Before *

Every day I woke up wishing that I could discover something new. Every night I went to bed hoping for a better tomorrow. According to the books I managed to scrounge, the rest of the world was full of passion and adventure. Somewhere over the horizon, there were interesting people. Challenges beyond matching gray thread to rough gray fabric.

But in my dull little village of Glenbert, each day stretched out as if time itself were sucking the color and life from it.

Perhaps it was that my father had rationed my food even more severely, and I was becoming exhausted. Perhaps it was working fourteen-hour days now. Or perhaps it was the shifty glances from the townsfolk finally wearing me down.

It was hard to believe that my own father would spread rumors that I was some sort of simpleton. All because I wouldn't marry the man he had attempted to betroth me to. Now he was also calling me a trollop, which was completely senseless since he was still trying to find a man to wed me.

Even at the tender age of nineteen years old, life had already beaten me down to the point where I did not dare to dream of anything better. Yet even with my horrid, dismal, passionless life, I could not bring myself to marry Thomas Glazenby, a rich yet disturbing man in his fifties.

I would not be traded simply to have my father in the Glazenby family's good graces. I could not build a life with a man who wanted nothing more than to practically tether me to his home so that I may do his bidding and bear his children.

Women rarely had the chance to stand up for themselves, but there must be a way to have a tiny shred of my own life.

I almost dreamed of being a schoolteacher like my mother had been long ago. I would love to teach children how to read, and develop a love of stories. But my father said it would not bring in enough money to pay for my food and clothing.

I almost dreamed of working in the bakery, as I'd always loved to cook. But my father had said that the baker's family were from the bad neighborhood over the river and had a terrible reputation.

Occasionally I was concerned with my own reputation. My father seemed to take every opportunity to spread lies about me to whoever would listen. I had never dared enter the pub where the men would drink ale and spin their tales until they were blurry. I knew how easily tales became lies. How some men longed to appear rich with knowledge, and faked it for the sake of holding the attention of the table.

A few times when I was feeling particularly brave, I would sneak out at night and hide under the open windows of the alehouse. My imagination would swim while listening to the adventures of the men who had sailed farther than we could ever have seen from the docks.

There were towns and cities so far away that the people had different foods. Different clothing. It sounded like some people were very rich, and had money to spend on frivolous things like decorative hats and exotic teas from the far East.

My heart ached for the opportunity to meet someone from afar. It had always been difficult for me to make conversation, as I'd always been the quiet sort. But maybe I could be brave enough to ask questions. How I would love to learn about these other lands.

Instead, I worked with my mother, sewing the most basic clothing, sheets, slipcovers, and staples for the local shops. I was surrounded by piles of cream, gray, and black fabric at all times. I swore to myself that someday I would fashion a brightly colored dress, like the wealthy women wore on Sundays. Yet I would wear mine for no occasion at all.

I almost dared to dream of a day and a place where I could have a bit of room to breathe freely. A life without every action analyzed by my overbearing father and his archaic views.

I knew that I was a nice girl. Proper, polite, and quiet. Exactly what I'd been taught. There was nothing shameful in wanting to learn about the world. Books were not sinful, and neither was asking questions of the neighbors and their travels. I was getting tired of having to cover my tracks and sneak around just to cross town to borrow a book, or trade buttons with a fellow seamstress.

I didn't know at what point I would be allowed to live my own life. There were rumors that the Langston brothers were finishing their schooling, and at least one of them would be coming back to the village. I could well imagine that my father would latch onto them immediately, and try once again to marry me off.

My shyness was frustrating enough with people I knew fairly well, and ran into at the market. Suddenly being handed to a strange man to… I couldn't even finish the thought. I knew at some point I'd be married and have to give myself to a man. Of all the outlandish dreams I tried to sweep out of my mind, the hope for a nice, honorable man who would be kind to me was the most important of all.

Mother had been married off to father to join their parent's properties together, back in the day. I don't recall ever seeing my mother give a genuine smile to my father. It was heartbreaking.

Longing for a life of laughter, and bright colors, and new adventures… I may as well have wished for the moon itself.

As the pale blue-white orb began to peek up over the horizon, I looked down at the darkened docks from my tiny bedroom window. I tried to think of its faint light as a beacon to the outside world. For the thousandth time, I wished upon the moon. Although I knew it was a silly superstition, I wished for the chance for a bigger, better life.

The moon ignored me, rising slowly over the sea.

***

~ Chapter 1 ~ Flora ~

The Village of Glenbert

I knew that if I didn't get my errands done quickly enough, I might get the lash again. My father had been even angrier than usual lately. I tried to seem invisible and stay out of his way.

Yet as I passed the plain gray shops full of plain gray faces along the main street of our village, I heard a rustle in the usual chatter. I walked more quickly, concentrating as I tried to listen.

The butcher was telling his wife about something down at the docks. The cobbler was out on his step asking old Mr. Laird if something was true. Finally I passed the blacksmith, his voice loud and hoarse from hovering over the heat of his forge for years. I heard a word that shot through me like a static shock on a dry winter day.

Pirates.

I'd heard the tales. The whispers during the day, and the loud, drunken stories from villagers at night. Ragged men who traveled with the winds. Men who took what they wanted, sailed where they liked, and lived completely free upon the seas.

The idea of going anywhere beyond my village thrilled me. Terrified me. Excited me to bits. The blood ran faster in my veins just from the mere thought of it.

I was desperate to leave this tired place, but I was under the thumb of my cruel, overbearing father. After I refused to be married off to Mr. Glazenby, a prissy, sickly, but very rich shopkeeper, my father threatened to disown me. He said that I was a burden, even though I worked even more hours every day than my poor mother, who taught me to be a seamstress as well.

The thought of spending a lifetime with someone who only saw me as a possession filled my throat with acid. I'd sooner jump into the sea myself than see my life handed over to another. I'd been starting to squirrel away a few meager pennies here and there, tucked under a floorboard beneath my bed. Someday I might find passage to another town where I could live freely. It was so risky that I didn't dare to even truly dream that it could happen.

Father's punishments were getting worse every time, and I wasn't quite sure how many more I could withstand.

Yet I risked a shred of his wrath to take the longer path home, that swung near the docks. If there were real pirates in our tiny village, I just had to steal a glimpse for myself.

Under the guise of pretending to look for my mother, who occasionally came to the shore before supper to buy a few fresh fish, I strolled as near as I dared.

There it was. A strange ship I'd never seen. There had been large cargo ships at our modest docks before. Although this particular ship wasn't the largest, it was different, somehow. Sleeker. It looked more predatory.

The enormous sails were down, but the proud masts and glistening wooden hull showed that it was easily the most interesting ship that had ever come to port. Several men in rough work clothes scrubbed the deck and coiled thick ropes. I couldn't quite believe that even though they were in poor repair, some of their shirts were bright colors like green and red.

Nobody in Glenbert would be so showy as to wear color except on Sundays, or perhaps to a fancy party, which only happened once a year. Here it was Wednesday, and a man with shining gold teeth wore a violet shirt to lug supplies onto the ship.

There were only four men, or quite possibly pirates, in

sight. I wondered how many it took to run such a vessel. I didn't know very much about ships and boats, or their workings. Then another man came up onto the deck, shielding his eyes from the sun for a moment with his hand.

His shirtless torso was glistening with a light sheen of sweat, and his black hair hung with the faintest curl at the ends. One of his thick, muscular arms was decorated with black ink, as well as an emblem on his chest. I wished that I was much closer so I could study the artwork. How does a person choose drawings that they would have with them forever?

I'd always dreamed of worldly men. Those who had seen distant places, learned the ways of other lands. So many exotic foods and towns and people. The excitement must be exhilarating.

From the way the great man was calling out commands to the other men, he must have been the Captain. Tearing my eyes from his massive shoulders, I pretended to scan the docks for my mother, just in case anyone noticed me.

Turning to go back up the path, I heard a slight shuffling and a thump. Glancing behind me, the Captain was down on the dock, picking up a huge barrel as easily as if it were empty, but it was likely fresh supplies.

For one blissfully exciting, horrifying, desperate second, he turned and his eyes met mine. They were so dark they seemed black. Yet they weren't savage or cruel. He laughed cheerily, giving me a nod as he raised his hand in a wave, then spun to carry the cargo onto his ship.

My hands fluttered, nearly dropped the bags of turnips, cabbage, and sewing thread. Rushing home, I stored the food and went straight back to work in my room, up by the window. I told my parents that it was the best light for my detailed work. In truth, I simply needed the fresh air and to look down at the docks, thinking of those who could sail away from this tiresome place.

When my fingers finally stopped shaking from excitement, I set to work, mending the butcher's wife's best dress with tiny, perfectly even stitches. With all of the hours I'd spent cutting, pinning, and sewing dresses, I knew that my work was the best in the village. Even faster and more accurate than my mother's, though I'd never breathe that to a soul.

After a spell, I found myself gazing out the window down to the men on the docks as they scurried about. It was likely all routine to them – winding ropes and tying sails. But to a young girl who had never been anywhere else, it was terribly exciting. Almost romantic.

"Why aren't you working?" Father's voice rang through the room, scaring me to pieces. "Staring out the window instead of tending to your chores? I should take the lash to you again."

Father's voice always set my teeth on edge, but today he seemed even more unstable.

He went to the window to see where I'd been looking. "Staring at the dock men like a harlot? You little..." He stopped mid-thought as he looked further to where the relatively large ship was docked at the end of our tiny harbor. "Pirates," he hissed. "In our nice village." He likely focused on the men working on deck, then back to my terrified eyes.

"If you'd been a son, you'd be doing real work like those men," he spat. "Now you bring shame to this house by ogling scoundrels and thieves."

His face was becoming red, and I heard my mother creep through the doorway. She likely heard his raised voice. I wasn't sure if her presence would protect me this time.

"You're unmarried at nineteen years of age. What's worse, you think you're too good for the nice man I arranged for you. You're a useless spinster. Do you have any idea what sort of vile gossip your poor mother must endure each time she goes to the market?"

I bit my lip to stop from reminding him that he was the only person who ever spread stories about me. Everyone else in the village pitied me, I was pretty sure. His complete lack of logic, and the way his moods turned on a penny, made most of the townspeople avoid him entirely.

Then father's clenched eyes shifted as he smiled wickedly. "Change into your nice new black dress. We're leaving in five minutes." He spun on his heel and bolted out the door.

Although we had no idea what was happening, mother helped me dress as quickly as possible. Her hands shook as she helped me into the layers of ruffled fabric, fastening the long row of buttons down my back.

"Where is he taking me?" I asked, my throat tight.

"I have no idea." She'd always been meek, her voice never raised far beyond a whisper. No wonder father thought he could control her completely.

By the time we raced downstairs, father had his good hat and jacket on. "Say goodbye to your mother. You'll not see her again."

"Mother?" I cried, turning to reach out my hand to her. My arm was already gripped by father's strong hand as he roughly dragged me out the door.

"Waste of food. Waste of education. And time," he muttered as he marched me down the path. "I've always said that you were worthless."

From the fire in his eyes and the set of his jaw, I honestly wondered if he was going to kill me. There was a cliff just through the forest that was rumored to be a good place for tossing bodies, but that was believed to be just a scary story. Surely my own father couldn't throw me away like old scraps?

"Please," I begged, trying to keep my voice low and meek. "I was just watching the boats. I only took a tiny break to rest my fingers. I can learn how to work harder."

"No. You're a waste and a disgrace. Best to have you gone from this village completely. Now we'll see if you're worth at least a few coins." He looked me up and down as I skittered beside him. "Maybe one coin."

We were headed for the pier. Before I had any idea of what was happening, my boots clacked on the wooden slats, as I was half dragged to the very end.

Father stopped in front of the new ship. "Ahoy," he called out. "Would you travelers like to purchase an extra deckhand?"

My mouth was suddenly dry as paper, and my heart began to race. I'd heard rumors of parents selling their children, but I thought it was an act of desperation. Why would he want to be rid of me this badly? I knew he wished every day that I'd been a son, but how could he blame me for that?

Looking up at the beautiful ship, I saw the name painted proudly on the side. The Fortune's Favor. I didn't know how being sold as if I were a side of beef could be considered fortunate. Perhaps this time my father's attempts at tarnishing my reputation had simply hit a new low, and he would drag me back home soon.

But he looked awfully determined this time.

~ Chapter 2 ~ The Captain ~

The Village Docks

Whenever I heard a raised voice when we visited a small town, I assumed it was the local toughs trying to run us out. It made no sense, since we brought them goods they would never find in this area. Then we spent most of the money we got for the cargo at their shops laying in supplies. Why would we buy things if we were bent on thieving?

Then I heard what the man was saying. Pulling on my coat and striding out to the deck, my eyes widened with surprise at the girl being dragged behind an angry man. I did not approve of the way his fingers were obviously digging into her arm. And I did not approve of restraining a grown woman as if she were a child having a tantrum.

"What's this then?" I asked, stepping closer. From the way a few of the local dock men were gathering, this was not an everyday situation here.

"My tramp of a daughter has likely already been lusting after you. She's brought shame to our family by turning down a suitable husband. How many pieces of gold for a healthy young girl?"

The idea of trading and selling humans had always turned my stomach. I'd heard of families selling their slowest son. They'd keep the smart one to run the family business, and the biggest one to do the labor. I'd heard of families selling one child to save six more.

But to sell a perfectly good woman, to a total stranger? That was pure evil.

Leaning over the edge of the railing, I took a good look at the folk gathered. I could see a few of the fishermen from two towns over. They were digging in their coin purses and having a frantic whispered conversation while ogling the poor lass.

This man was throwing the poor girl away. If I didn't take her in, some unscrupulous bastard would.

Looking down at her wild, terrified eyes, I could see she wasn't a tramp. From the cut of his clothing and the size of his belly, the father wasn't starving.

I'd been mulling over the idea of one more crew member. I'd downsized the crew by more than half since we'd changed our ways. The idea of bringing a woman on board wasn't very common. However, it was sewing, mending, and cooking that we needed the most help with.

Reaching out my hand, I smiled as warmly as I could. "Come here, lass. Let's have a look at you."

Her delicate hand was trembling, but she took mine and walked up the plank to stand before me on the deck. I realized that my size seemed to frighten her a bit. There was no way to know what sort of tales she'd heard of sailors and our ways.

"I won't hurt you, little one," I said softly.

The way her eyes glanced up at me nervously, then jumped away was almost amusing, but I couldn't stand that I was terrifying her.

"What's your name, lass?" I said as gently as my gruff voice allowed.

"Flora," she said softly. Her voice was nearly carried away by the breeze. The poor thing seemed to be in a state of shock, and rightly so. In this backward town, she'd likely met very few strangers.

"She's quite the pretty little thing, and seems healthy," I announced.

Her father's eyes burned with hatred as he glared at her. "She's a disgrace to her family, and doesn't belong with decent folk."

I turned to raise an eyebrow sternly, until he realized his dangerous error. "I'm sorry, sir. Village folk. Er, you know what I mean."

The rest of my crew were howling with laughter, crowding closer to ogle the woman who might be joining our travels. Their amusement was shared by local dock men who were cautiously drawing closer to witness the entertainment.

"Boys, she's a beauty, ain't she?" I roared to the crew.

"Aye, Captain!" my five men hollered back.

"How many gold pieces would a lovely lassie like this be worth to ye?" I demanded. If I was going to shame this bastard of a man, I wanted to make a public spectacle of it that would follow him forever.

A darkly tanned man with gold teeth leered. "Her sweet blue eyes look so innocent. We'd have to teach her everything around here, Cap'n. Perhaps three gold pieces."

"Thank ye, Teeth. O'Doule, what say you?"

"That lovely white skin will sear in the sun, Captain. We'd have to keep her below decks most of the time. Three gold pieces."

"Dirty Davy?"

A tall, lanky man in a dusty gray headscarf stepped forward. "She's a tiny one, Cap'n, but I think I see a spark of gumption in 'er eyes. Five gold pieces. That be fair."

"Aye," called out a stocky man at the back. "Five be generous."

"Thank ye, McGee."

The poor lass looked like she wanted the sea to swallow her, and make her disappear. Having this talk in front of her was not very gentlemanly, I'd admit.

I looked behind me, searching out the last crewman. "Little Larry," I asked more gently, "What do you think of this delicate gal?"

A giant of a man, nearly seven feet tall with the well-worn face of a thug walked slowly forward. I was impressed that the girl didn't flinch. His gentle eyes examined her quite seriously. "May I see your hands, Miss?" he asked politely. She seemed a bit unnerved by his deep tone, but she lifted her hands to him.

Larry turned them so her palms were up, so careful it was if he were afraid of hurting her. Bending forward, he examined her fingertips. "She can sew, Cap'n. Likely quite well, as she's put in many hours. She could help me make our new sails, and clothing."

He let her hands fall. Then he wrapped his fingers around her waist, determining how much of her silhouette was from the puffed layers of her dress, and how tiny her slender body was within. His huge hands completely encircled her. "She's a bit thin, Cap'n. She won't require much food at all, but we should likely try to fatten her up just a hair. We'll need her to become a bit more sturdy to survive the winter."

I was listening intently to every word. My first mate's opinion was the most important.

Larry tipped her face up with his finger to look deeply into her eyes. He lowered his voice even more so that only she and I could hear him. "She's not afraid of us, specifically. She's afraid of the whole world. Someone has told her she's worthless, and she doesn't realize how lovely she is."

I nodded, contemplating. "And your price, mate?"

"Seven gold pieces, Cap'n," Larry announced. Flora gasped in shock, then quickly stared down at her feet. Larry stepped back to join the crew at a respectful distance. A crowd had been steadily gathering on the pier, and the villagers gasped as well.

With that, he had told me that he wanted to keep her, and that she would be a good addition to the crew. Larry and I had always had a way of communicating through subtleties.

I nodded, thinking. The rumors I'd heard of people selling their children said they never fetched a price of more than five gold pieces. Looking down at the dock, the father shifted his weight nervously, possibly ashamed at having underestimated his daughter's worth. I hoped that he feared the judgment of the townsfolk for selling her in the first place.

"Thank you, Little Larry," I said, still contemplating. "I'm going to steal her away for a quick parlay. You stay put," I ordered her father. Then I glanced at my men with a nod, signalling for them to keep watch.

I took Flora's hand, leading her to the far side of the ship, behind a stack of cargo bales for a moment. "My men like you," I said, low enough so that only she could hear. "I would never bring a soul aboard my vessel they didn't trust. Little Larry likes you very much, and his opinion means the world to me. You do sew, then?"

She nodded. "Yes, sir. I've been working hard since I was small. I could easily outfit your entire crew with the proper supplies, and I can repair things so well that they'll hold up for years." She leaned closer, reaching to examine a tear on the collar of my coat.

Her hair smelled so fresh, like a spring breeze. Her delicate skin looked as silky as a rose petal. Yet her bright blue eyes, so clear with concentration, told me that she was a woman who could stay on task.

She was so focused on the fabric that she didn't realize her proximity to me. "I could fix this within an hour..."

Then her hands snapped away. She looked up at me shyly, and a lower man would have snuck a kiss. I realized this innocent young girl needed protection. She needed someone to show her the ways of the world. From the way my heart began to thud unevenly in my chest, I needed it to be me.

"Did ye know 'tis lucky to touch a sailor's collar?" She shook her head. "I think it's a sign, sweet girl."

Her long light hair, big blue eyes, and pale, rounded face made her look like a porcelain doll. Yet it was the way her gaze darted around the ship that made me truly take notice. She was curious. Smart. A gal like this would be interesting to have around.

Reaching out, I tucked a stray tendril of soft hair back behind her ear, letting my fingertips graze her cheekbone. "I've never seen a lass so beautiful."

Somehow her tiny sigh, soft as a whisper, reached my ears. I could plainly see her wide pupils, how her breath trembled with each exhale. The lass enjoyed being this close to me. I was intrigued. It had been a long time since I'd been with a woman, and even longer still that I'd considered keeping one around for more than a few nights.

For the moment, I decided, I'd bring her along and see what developed.

"Do you want to come with us for a life of adventure?"

She bit that perfect full bottom lip. Then she gave me the softest smile. "You're the first person who has ever asked me what I wanted, sir."

My heart may have broken for her, but for the fact her sweetness was warming me clear through. She looked off into the distance, contemplating only for a second. "Yes, please, sir."

"You'll obey me, serve me, serve my crew and this ship?"

"Yes, sir."

I nodded, a wide smile overtaking me. "You have no idea what a treasure you truly are, lassie. Now be a good girl and play along while we humiliate that rotten father of yours, yes?" She nodded very seriously.

I took her arm gently, and marched her back to where her father waited impatiently. The crowd of townsfolk had tripled. It was my duty as an honorable man to shame the townie bastard of a father who would treat a good woman this way.

I stood beside Flora so all could see her clearly. The glow of the setting sun ignited the gold of her hair, and warmed her delicate skin.

The villagers seemed to take a careful look at her, as if for the first time. She was radiant, beautiful. I had a deep instinct that she was kind. Why hadn't anyone tried to help her escape that man before?

"So, since her father is throwing away a perfectly good daughter, we've determined that we'll take her." The townsfolk who still weren't sure what was happening all gasped in shock. Selling one's daughter to a pirate, or any kind of sailor? Horrified whispers ran through the crowd like a brushfire.

"There has, however, been some discrepancy as to the price. What is a fine young girl worth? My men seem to think that she might be worth five gold pieces. Some say as high as seven." The murmurs silenced, as every person assembled was dying to hear the verdict first hand. This was the sort of tale they'd be telling their grandchildren. They likely wanted to get every detail correct.

"A pretty little lass like this, with flaxen hair and eyes as blue as the sea itself. A girl who can mend, and sew, and immediately offered to fix my coat without being asked." A few of the older ladies laughed, but were quickly shushed. "A brave girl who wishes to set out on the open sea for a world of adventure rather than be trapped under the thumb of a father who despises her, and has told her she's worthless."

The father looked like he'd rather slink away empty-handed than face further humiliation, but he was trapped by my poisonous glare.

"I asked Flora what she herself wanted. She declared she'd rather sail away with us than stay here with her family."

An older woman gasped, her hand flying up to cover her mouth. The crowd murmured for a moment, then became silent again.

I paused. This was not a time to make a deal. This was a time to make a point. This poor little lass might consider her absolute worthiness by this exchange. Looking over at her hopeful face, I wanted her to know that she was a precious thing. All women were, of course, but she was a treasure all her own.

"A lass with all of these grand qualities, with a heart full of passion, is worth all of the gold in the world." I reached into an interior coat pocket, drawing out a small black bag that jangled heavily. "But instead, I'll give all of the gold I have in my coat. Twenty gold pieces."

The silence of the crowd was absolute, but for a few stifled gasps. That was a years' salary for a lucky, hard-working man, and more than some would see in all of their days.

Flora's mouth fell open, her bottom lip trembling as she looked up at me. Her little fingers gripped her skirt in fists. Then her head shook slightly as if she couldn't believe it.

Leaning down to whisper in her ear, I allowed my lips to brush her skin as I breathed, "If I'd had it handy, I'd have paid ten times as much to keep you safe, sweet girl."

She blinked hard, her sky blue eyes filling with tears. Yet I couldn't tell if it was from gratitude, relief, or confusion.

Standing up straight, I tossed the bag and a wicked glare to her father, who caught both clumsily.

"There is only one demand I must make." The father nodded for me to continue, unable to meet my eyes again. I turned to the townsfolk, who all looked as shocked as if I'd slapped them. "You will tell her mother what transpired here today. Do not let the disgrace of this horrid man be forgotten. He might be temporarily rich, but he'll be a spineless, cruel bastard forever."

The father slunk a few steps down the boards of the walkway with his sack of gold, burning with shame under the glares of his neighbors.

"Set sail, lads. We're off." My men scurried around, raising the sails, securing the fresh cargo, and hauling up the anchor.

I stood beside Flora, placing a gentle hand on her shoulder, guiding her to the railing at the stern. "Take a last look, lassie. We might never be back." I noticed that her eyes locked with her father's, where he stood directly beneath her on the pier. Lowering my voice, I said, "Any last words for that despicable man?"

Without hesitation, she spat hard – the saliva catching him full in the face. He bucked backward, tripping over some ropes, falling on his arse painfully as the villagers roared with laughter. He clutched his sack of gold to his chest, staring at his daughter as if she had stabbed him.

Flora turned on her heel, walking to the other end of the ship so she would never have to look at him again.

I was completely impressed by her sass, and followed her, now laughing hard and loud. "Lass, I must say, that was the best goodbye and good riddance I've seen in all my years. I have never been so proud of a gal in my life."

She walked all the way up to the bow, leaning on the polished wood of the railing, her shoulders shaking. I came up behind her, not sure what to do. Relying on instinct, I wrapped her in my thick arms, pulling her further away from the dock, and the stares of the townspeople.

She spun, leaning her cheek against my shirt as the sobs overtook her. Rocking her gently, I murmured to her softly as she cried as if she were being torn apart. I tried not to smell her luscious hair, and think about the softness of her delicate form in my grasp. When her body finally stopped quaking, I rubbed her back, and whispered into her ear, "You're the bravest little lass I've ever seen. I promise to keep you safe."

Flora stepped back, perhaps realizing that she'd just broken down in front of a stranger. "I'm so sorry, sir. I don't... this is so unlike me." She tried hard to catch her breath and compose herself. "I don't even know you. To be so familiar... I'm terribly sorry, sir."

"Lass, you're soon going to learn about me, the boys, and the workings of this ship. We won't be strangers for long. There is much to learn. It is a strange life to adjust to. I'll be here to hold you if ever you need it."

Looking down into her soft eyes, it felt like she was still trembling. This poor, sheltered little gal was about to spend her first night away from home, and was likely frightened to bits. All she could manage was a slight nod of her head.

I put an arm around her, turning us to face north, and pointed to a light starting to rise above the water. "Do you know what that is?" I pointed.

"The north star, sir."

"I knew you were a clever girl."

She smiled, seeming embarrassed. It broke my heart how she seemed unnerved by a compliment.

"We need to plot our course for the next few days, and the boys have a lot of work to do before dark. There are no extra hammocks down in the bunk room, and I cannot let a delicate lass sleep anywhere but a proper bed. However, the only bed on board is my own."

Her wide eyes were so beautiful, even as she looked terrified. I chuckled softly, which seemed to calm her. "Don't panic, lassie. You'll be sleeping in my bed, but I won't be ravishing you. I'm going to care for you."

Her blue eyes widened again, but then she nodded resolutely. "You've purchased me, sir. I am yours to do with what you will."

I took her hands in mine, and looked at her quite seriously. "You'll have to share my bed, but I won't be touching you. I think it's best if you get your sea legs, and learn about the workings of this ship, for your own safety. Alright?"

She released a long breath, visibly relieved. "Yes, sir."

"Right. I'm going to hand you over to Little Larry, and he can show you around the ship while I go over some charts with O'Doule."

"Thank you, sir."

I grinned, unable to resist running my thumb along her fair cheek. "I'm Captain Samuels. But I must admit, I rather like being called sir."

She blushed, perhaps not used to this much attention. Lifting her skirts slightly to step over the ropes and down the steps, she followed me as quickly as she could.

~ Chapter 3 ~ Flora ~

** The Fortune's Favor **

What have I done? Or should I say, what has happened to me? I had no choice, but still, I had to wonder. Would the Captain have still taken me on board had I tried to refuse? It was hard to say.

He actually seemed like a decent man. I took notice that he tried to soften his tone with me, and not frighten me more than need be. Those deep eyes made me feel completely drawn to him, in an oddly exciting way. His thick arms and massive chest made me feel something new. Something deep, and strange.

Although a part of me felt humiliated for crying in his arms, it was reassuring that he comforted me. Even now, as he took my hand to help me step down to the lower deck without tripping on my skirts, his focus seemed to be on keeping me safe, and nothing else.

Though his face was rugged, he was incredibly striking as he said with a huge grin, "Flora, this is Little Larry, our first mate."

I smiled as I looked up at the enormous man. He had very short dark hair, warm brown eyes, and a noticeable scar that ran straight across his cheek to where a large part of the top of his ear was missing. Carefully looking only at his eyes, I held out my hand politely. He shook mine gently. "Hello, Larry."

"Hello, Miss. Nice to officially meet you."

"Larry, I need to go over the charts with O'Doule. Could you show Flora around, introduce her to the boys, and I'll meet you in the galley shortly?"

"Aye, sir."

The second the Captain left, Larry gave me a cautious smile. "Miss, you're a brave girl to join a ragged crew like this. Have you been on a ship before?"

"Not a real ship, sir, never."

He looked amused, then his warm brown eyes softened. "Titles are much more casual on The Fortune's Favor. Only the Captain is 'sir', Miss. I'm just Larry."

"I'm sorry I nearly giggled when he called you Little Larry."

"It's okay," he chuckled. "Half of the crew does."

He began leading me to the back of the ship, pausing as I stepped carefully over some coiled ropes.

"Miss, tomorrow we might need to shorten your skirts." I must have made an expression of surprise, as he laughed lightly. "No, Miss, not to be cheeky. Just a few inches so that they don't get filthy dragging around the deck, and so you don't trip on ropes, or tools or the like."

"Oh. Of course."

"Or we might find you a pair of slops in the old clothing chest."

I nodded, though just the thought of wearing men's pants was exceedingly uncomfortable.

"There are many rules on this ship. Not falling overboard is pretty much number two, after no thievin' from crewmates."

I nodded, trying not to laugh. "Okay."

"But if you do fall into the water, be sure to scream bloody murder on the way down."

That sounded strange. "You don't scream after you're in the water?"

"Then too, yes. But you might be knocked out, or the cold water might seize up your lungs for a second. So if you ever think you're going over, scream quick and loud. We can't fish you out if we're miles away by the time we know you're missing."

I nodded. "That's sensible."

Looking around, two of the men were beginning to hoist the sails, and we were already gliding away from the dock. I wasn't used to men punching each other on the shoulders, and acting so rough. But this was their home, and nobody should change because a girl like me was here.

"Miss, I feel that I need to tell you something. It might be awkward, but I see that you're a bit nervous around all of these men."

I nodded, noticing how the corner of Larry's eyes tightened, not wanting to say whatever it was he felt he needed to share.

"None of the boys will touch you, Miss. I assure you, if any of the lads ever grabs you, it would be to save you from a swinging boom, or to stop you from tripping on the deck ropes. You're under the protection of the Captain, which makes you a member of this crew. So even if the lads get rowdy and mouthy, you should know that you're safe."

I smiled up at him, genuinely relieved at this news, and touched that the giant would be so thoughtful. "Thank you," I nodded. "I truly appreciate that."

"I've been the Captain's first mate for several years, Miss, and he's a good man. But if you ever need to ask questions and he's not around, I am at your service." His deep scar creased higher as he grinned. "I'll be very grateful with the stitchin' help. I'm the only one with the patience to try my hand at it, but my hands..." He held one up. "Not really those of a seamstress."

I laughed, too loudly, I thought, but my voice was caught by the breeze and flew away. "I really have been sewing for years. Perhaps tomorrow you can give me a pile of work, and I can start earning my keep right away."

"Deal," he said, shaking my lily-white palm in his huge, tanned hand.

Larry gave me a quick tour of the mid decks. "You'll have to learn a few things quickly, Miss. The back of the ship is the stern, the front is the bow. Instead of left and right, which switches depending on which way you're facing, we have port and starboard."

He pointed, and I tried to think of the ship as a sketch in one of my geography books. "So if you're facing the bow, the front," I said, thinking, "Starboard would be the right."

"Yes," he smiled.

"And left is port."

"Correct."

"Port and left both have four letters. Starboard and right both have more letters." Larry's mouth fell open, but I continued. "As you sail away, people on the dock would give stern glances that you left them behind. When you bow to the King, you bow forward. So that all makes sense."

Larry blinked with what appeared to be shock. "You're very quick, Miss. The Fortune's Favor is a sloop – that's the style of the ship. We're able to run her with just six crewmen, or even less, since these men are all rather skilled." His eyes suddenly sparkled in delight. "You're lucky number seven, Miss."

I grinned back at him, relieved that speaking with these strange men was getting easier. I'd been painfully shy my whole life, but now it was almost like I was outside myself looking in. Could I be a new person if I was in a different place?

Larry led me across the decks, pointing out various features and dangers. I jumped when I heard a thump, and spun to see two of the men salute to the Captain, who had just appeared in the doorway.

I turned west to see the last trails of orange and red streak across the enormous sky. I was in a new world of color now, where I could take a moment to enjoy the sunset without fear of being punished. Where people seemed to want to teach me, just for the sake of keeping me safe, and sharing knowledge.

As I turned back to Larry, he smiled warmly. "Yes, Miss. You'll see that the sky is far bigger out here. I'd say you'll get used to it, but I never have."

Another thump made me jump, nearly squealing.

"Easy, lass," the Captain said. He was suddenly behind

me, and I noticed that Larry instantly took a step back. "I want you to take one last look at Glenport."

Turning to see the hills of my home town growing smaller and dimmer, I could barely make out the dark blob with a brightly lit top window that used to be my house.

The Captain's heavy hand rested on my shoulder. "Are you okay so far, lass?"

"Yes, sir. I promise you, I won't get homesick."

His chuckle blended with Larry's. "Aye, that I don't doubt."

"She already knows her ship directions, sir," Larry said, seeming proud.

"Good girl. You two get down to the galley, and I'll join the crew in a few minutes."

"Aye, Captain."

Larry went down the steep steps first, reaching out to hold my hand so that if I fell, he'd catch me. It was slightly odd that these strange men were more caring and considerate in my first hour of knowing them than my father had been my entire life.

Most of the crew were already settled around a round wooden table, and Larry pulled out a barrel for me to sit on. "Flora, this is the crew," Larry said. "McGee is the one stirring the stew, but maybe tomorrow you could help him with the cooking."

A short, slightly portly man with a wide mustache turned to give me a nod. "Miss."

"Nice to meet you," I nodded back.

"This 'ere's Teeth, obviously," Larry grinned.

I smiled back at the wiry man flashing three front teeth of gold.

"And I'm Davy," said the strong-looking younger man with a gray scarf around his head.

The other men shot him a glance until Teeth grinned, "That's Dirty Davy. Keep your distance, Miss. We've been told that he's not bathed this year."

"Lies and half-truths with this lot," he grinned saucily to

me, leaning in. "Ye best not believe half of what these beggars tells ya."

"Aye, and here's O'Doule," Larry said quickly, nodding to an older man with spectacles. He looked hardy, nearly as strong as the rest. "He's the one who reads the maps and charts, and knows the details and histories of the places we visit."

I reached out to shake his hand. "Lovely to meet you, O'Doule."

"Miss Flora," he smiled warmly. "Welcome to The Fortune's Favor. I'm sorry the circumstances were a little… untoward. But you're just in time for some quick voyages to rather beautiful, elegant towns. Some towns are more picturesque than others, you'll find."

Teeth rolled his eyes. "He's a poet, that one. Loves to stare at old buildings even more than the girls and the treasures."

"I'd like to learn a little history of the places we visit, if you don't mind," I said softly. He had to lean in to hear me.

"Certainly, Miss. It'll be nice to teach someone." O'Doule nodded to me, then took a bowl and plate from McGee and left the galley. In a moment, the Captain returned, and I realized that the men must be taking turns at the wheel.

As soon as the Captain sat down beside me, McGee served dinner. It was a light stew with lots of fresh vegetables, and bread that was obviously from Miss Celena's bakery.

"We eat light the first day out of port, so that tomorrow seems like a feast," the Captain explained. "We'll only be out five days but it's our way. That gives us a better idea of how to ration our supplies as well."

I nodded. "I don't need much food, really," I said quickly. "I'm grateful for whatever you can spare."

The men seemed to glance around at each other, and I noticed a few frowns.

"Here," Teeth said, slipping an extra slice of bread onto my plate. "Larry was right as you came on board. You could do with a bit more food. And I don't much like the dark grainy stuff anyway."

"Thank you very much," I whispered, devouring every morsel. This was the first time in my life I didn't feel judged for every bite I consumed.

I noticed the Captain giving me an encouraging smile and nod. "That's right, lassie. You eat as much as you need. It gets cold in the fall before we head south, and you'll need a bit of meat on those little bones."

During dinner, the men got a bit rowdy, drinking deeply from their tin mugs. I sipped water from mine, even though Larry offered me a taste of his.

"No, thank you," I said, hoping I didn't offend him.

"Are you such a fancy lady that you don't drink the devil's water with the rest of us?" laughed Davy.

"No," I said quickly. "I've just never had it before. And as it's my first night here, I don't want to fall overboard quite yet." The men laughed uproariously.

Larry beamed. "Captain, you realize she makes this a seven-person crew?"

I turned to see his eyes grow wide. "Aye, you're right." The Captain flashed me a wide grin. "She also touched my ripped collar without knowing what that meant."

Teeth and Davy clanked their mugs together.

"That's good luck indeed," McGee said, wiping rum from his mustache. "Maybe with her as a lucky charm, we should look into running the straits with a load of–"

"That's not dinner table conversation," the Captain said, cutting him off. "We'll see what's what after we visit Parrinport."

His head snapped up. "Bugger it. O'Doule was right. The wind changed."

He stood up quickly. "I'll be back shortly," the Captain said to me before dashing from the room.

Larry explained, "We're near a few relatively narrow passages, Miss. We're totally safe, but the Captain wants to make sure our course is clear for Teeth and Davy to steer as they take the night shifts."

"Well," Teeth drawled, "You'll be safe on my watch.

Come sunrise, who knows where Dirty Davy will have us."

"Don't you start," Davy sneered with a lopsided grin. "I'm not the one who nearly bottomed us near Fleeryville."

Larry and McGee both rolled their eyes, and the conversation went on for quite some time about who had a steadier hand at the wheel.

I listened to every word with rapt attention. These men were already treating me like a friend, as one of their own. It was fascinating that they seemed to enjoy my company. This was the loudest, rowdiest, most wonderfully impolite dinner I'd ever attended, and I felt more welcomed than I ever had at my table at home.

~ Chapter 4 ~ The Captain ~

* *Stars* *

"You haven't had your say yet," I said to O'Doule as I met him by the wheel.

"Did you want my honest opinion?" he said carefully, raising one eyebrow in the lamplight.

"Always. You know that."

O'Doule pretended to think very hard for a moment, but then his grin slipped out. "I think she's lovely, captain. I hate to say that she might need to toughen up a bit, but I think the boys will help her."

He paused, regarding me carefully. "And you know, the timing is impeccable. With a delicate, proper lass such as Flora, it will certainly help sell the image that we are a respectable trading outfit. She could pose as a passenger if need be."

I nodded. "Although that was never my intention, the same thought had crossed my mind."

O'Doule shrugged as he laid out the maps. "Killing two birds with one stone," he said.

"What do you have against birds?" I asked. "That's a terrible saying. How about, feeding two birds with one seed?"

O'Doule smirked. "If I didn't have my personal safety in mind, Captain, I would say that the pretty lass has softened you already."

I waved my finger in his face but could never really be angry with my navigator. "You know where mouthiness will get you. Know how to make this foolproof for the boys on watch tonight?"

We finished the calculations quickly, and I sent O'Doule back down to the galley. I simply needed a moment to myself. Looking out the window up at the thousands upon thousands of stars, I realized that they did not compare to Flora's delicate beauty.

The feelings I already had for the clever girl surprised me. I never thought that I'd find a woman who truly warmed my heart. Yet Flora felt like she already lived there, nestled into my chest like a secret treasure.

I'd have to learn to be careful, and let her open up to me. She was obviously a sweet, innocent girl, and there was no way I could allow her to be hurt or upset. I also couldn't let her think that she was a possession. I wanted her to be a crewman in her own right. Crew woman. Bugger it, I'd have to work on that.

From the second my eyes met hers, I felt something completely new. I needed to protect her. Comfort her. Take care of her in every possible way. I wasn't the sort of man who ever considered falling to a woman's feet, but if she asked, I would in a heartbeat.

Yet I also wanted to teach her. Show her the world. Gaze upon the sunset reflecting in her eyes as she sailed with us for new lands.

That likely sounded far more romantic than it would actually be. Our next three trips would be back and forth between Parrinport and Leelard Island, ferrying various not quite legal kegs and certain slightly underground trade items.

I'd been toying with the decision to focus more on smuggling than outright theft. When an opportunity arose for many of the old crew bent on piracy to move on to a new ship, it was fortunate indeed.

Larry agreed that trading and shipping would be both safer and more lucrative in the long run. With the military wanting to show off their power by taking down pirates, there came a day when a man wanted semi-honest work to cut down on the pesky annoyance of being chased all the time.

We'd even been talking of hoisting a new flag with no hint of a skull or bones. Each Captain had their own flag, and there must be a way to have something that states we are powerful without being nasty.

Studying the stars above me, I hoped the men wouldn't be disturbed by Flora's presence on the ship. Throwing off the balance of the men just when I had assembled a great small crew was not ideal, but there was no way I could have left her for some bastard to purchase. The men knew that.

***

~ Chapter 5 ~ Flora ~

** The Captain's Quarters **

I realized I hadn't had a meal this delicious in a long time. I also saw that everyone's bowls and plates were empty. "Shall I begin washing up?" I asked softly, looking at McGee. Then I saw that the Captain had appeared in the doorway.

"No, lass, you can start helping tomorrow," the Captain said. "Tonight we'll go have a chat and get you settled."

Another strange glance flashed from man to man around the table. I wondered what they were thinking. Then I realized that they might be wondering about the bed sharing situation. My hands began to flutter as I realized I was wondering too.

"All right men. Don't get too rowdy tonight. There is a heap and a half of work tomorrow. I'll be turning in now."

I looked up and saw him tilt his head to indicate that I should follow. "Goodnight," I whispered to Larry, nodding to the rest of the men as I scurried away at the Captain's heels.

Taking a deep breath as I followed the tall man, I tried to appear calm. I knew I'd likely be the talk of the evening around that table as the drinking went on. I was accustomed to being the talk of the town, due to rumors that my father spread. But this time the gossip might have an edge closer to the truth. I had no way of knowing.

The Captain led me into a room at the other end of the ship, far away from the galley and the bunk room.

I'd never slept anywhere but my own tiny bed. The thought of sleeping in a hammock in a room full of men was too much to contemplate. I realized how kind the Captain was to take me in, but I couldn't help wondering what he had in mind.

He had purchased me. I belonged to him now. So he could really do anything he liked.

As he opened the door, I stepped into a small wooden room. It was furnished with a small bed, several clothing hooks on the walls, and a few built-in shelves. The scent of the wood weathered by the salty sea air was comforting.

"You may wear one of my shirts to sleep in," the Captain said matter of factly. "It shall hang like a dress on you, and will be appropriate enough. At our next port of call, you and Larry can pick up any fabric you need to make yourself some new clothing." He handed me a huge but soft old linen shirt.

I set it on the bed as I removed my shoes, then awkwardly looked down at the floor.

"Oh, I'm sorry lass," the Captain said, "You have my word that I will not look." He sat on the edge of the bed with his back to me.

"No, um, it's just that... I cannot reach the buttons along my back. My mother has always helped me dress."

He turned to me with an odd look in his eyes. I tried to hide my slight shaking as he said, "Let me help you."

I stepped in front of him, turning my back as I allowed him to undress me. He tried to work the tiny buttons faster with his thick fingers. Feeling his hands so close to my skin, and his warm breath down my neck, was making me flutter inside. "Calm down, sweet girl. Everything is fine." He fumbled at the bottom few fasteners, then finally freed me. As he opened the dress at the back so that I could remove the rest myself, I heard a savage growl.

I spun quickly. Did I displease him in some way? With tiny steps I began to inch away, looking over my shoulder at him.

His eyes were nearly black with rage as his fingertips lightly touched my shoulders. "Who put those marks on your back?"

"Oh, I forgot."

It looked like what he was seeing nearly broke something deep inside a man who had likely seen horrors beyond measure. He lowered his voice to a sharp whisper. "Who?"

"I... um, I angered my father a few times, sir. Especially two days ago."

"And he gave you the lash?" he asked, incredulous.

"He said that's what all parents did to bring up children right, sir. I learned my lessons quickly, or at least, I really tried. I almost always get things correct at the first try now, sir, really I do."

The anger emanating from him was incredible, and he looked like he could have punched through a stone wall. I nervously took another step back before he seemed to sense my fear.

Instantly he softened, holding out his hands. "Come here, little one. I'm not angry with you."

I slowly took the four steps forward to stand before him, extending my trembling hands. He held them gently, looking into my eyes with a softness that I would never have expected from what I assumed was a hardened criminal.

"Your father is a bad man," he said quietly. "I want you to know that you'll never be punished here. If you make a mistake, we'll correct you by simply telling you. The lash is reserved for men who steal from their mates, or act truly dishonorably. Do you understand?"

I didn't dare speak, just nodded.

"I don't want you to fear me," he continued. "You're mine now, and no harm will come to you." He reached out to cup my cheek in his large hand. I was deeply affected by the simple gesture. I tried not to let him see the shudder that ran through me as I realized I'd never been touched by a kind man.

"Do those cuts and bruises hurt?" he asked, his gruff voice soft.

"Not much. I'm used to it, sir." I noticed the corners of his eyes twitch, as if he couldn't stand the thought.

"Tomorrow you'll ask Larry for the salve, and have him

rub some onto your back. His scar was much worse before we treated him." I nodded. "Do you need any more help with your dress?"

"No, sir. Thank you."

"Okay, change quickly then." He turned away as I pulled off my dress, then the petticoats, and tugged on his giant shirt. "May I turn back?"

"Yes."

Sure enough, it was nearly a dress on me, but much more close-fitting than those fashionable ruffles. I realized that he could almost see the outline of my knickers right through it. I realized now that my frame was showing, my narrow waist was clear, which made my breasts and hips look curvier. Looking up shyly, I saw the Captain seem to tear his gaze away from my bosom.

He pulled back the blankets. "Get in." I obeyed immediately, slipping into his bed. It was actually softer than the one I'd had at home. But it wasn't very wide, and I realized with a flash of nervousness that it would be close quarters indeed.

He tugged off his shirt, and I found myself unable to look away for several blinks. That tan skin, broad chest, and layers of firm muscle all made me feel strange deep inside. The yearning to touch him was nearly overwhelming. He caught me admiring him just a second before I glanced away.

I remembered that it was my staring that had brought all of this about in the first place. He started to remove his pants, then paused, and seemed to change his mind.

Sliding in beside me, he tried to give me as much room as possible. "Snug as a bug?" he asked.

I liked that he wasn't nearly as fearsome as he looked, and was quick to laugh. "Yes, thank you."

"Do you have everything you need?"

It was odd that he was actually treating me like a guest. I was a possession, bought and paid for. Surely he couldn't be that generous, no matter what he said.

"Yes, but um... sir, is there anything you need?"

"What do you mean?"

I could feel my cheeks burning, but felt the question must be asked, even though it was barely a whisper. "Well, um... do you wish for me to… serve you in any way? To earn my keep?" I tucked my head so that he couldn't see me blushing, but forced myself to add, "Twenty gold pieces is an awful lot of money, sir. You must expect something in return, and it is my duty."

He turned toward me, leaning on his elbow. "My precious lass, they really mixed up your noggin, didn't they?"

"Sir?"

He shook his head. "Nobody should buy and sell people, sweet girl. We're pirates. Criminals. Or, we used to be. Yet even we know how revolting that is." He sighed heavily. "You were born in the wrong village, apparently. If you had better parents, in a different place, you'd be the girl who all of the men fought to court. You'd be the girl every other girl wanted to be. But your piece of shit father has bent your mind into thinking you're less than common."

My mouth fell open. No man had ever used that sort of language directly in front of me. He noticed my shock. "Dammit, I'm sorry. My tongue gets loose when I'm angry."

I nodded, hoping that he'd continue. My head was swimming with the thought that maybe I wasn't the lowest girl in the village for being an unmarried seamstress at nineteen. Was that even possible?

He smiled warmly. "I don't expect you to serve me in any way, lass, beyond being a useful member of the crew." He leaned closer, his thumb brushing a stray hair from my forehead. "I think you're the most beautiful woman I've ever seen," he said softly, staring into my eyes.

I couldn't speak. I felt a strange pressure in my chest, and a nervous pull toward him. He was so striking, so ruggedly handsome. He was the Captain of this great ship. Yet he seemed to have special feelings for me. It made no sense.

"You have every right to say no, little Flora, but I cannot resist asking. May I give you a kiss goodnight?"

My head bobbed too eagerly. I wondered if he could see that I was overwhelmed, stunned, and still a bit shaky. He brought his lips to mine gently, holding them there just for a moment before pulling away. My eyes fluttered back open, surprised by his tenderness.

"Goodnight, lassie," he said, turning over so his back was to me.

I turned the other way, pressing my lips together. Never in all my life would I have dreamed that my first kiss would be to a pirate Captain out on the open sea.

***

I woke up feeling a large hand gently stroking my hair. I released a soft sigh, curling against the warm body under me. My eyes slowly opened and I looked around, realizing where I was.

"Good morning, lassie," the Captain whispered.

I blinked awake, startled, then realized I was snuggled against his chest in a very familiar manner. "Oh," I gasped, sitting up and quickly shifting to the edge of the bed. As soon as I moved away, I wished I hadn't. His body against mine felt so… I didn't have the right words, just a huge mess of swirling feelings in my stomach.

The Captain laughed, completely unoffended. "Apparently in your sleep, you decided that my chest was softer than your pillow. I'll have to start hauling more barrels to toughen up."

I was appalled until I saw the gleam in his eye. He sat up and cupped my cheek in his palm. The touch caused my heart to race, as my eyes traveled up his powerful arms, and across his strong shoulders.

Noticing his eyes wander downward, I realized that the top button of the shirt I was wearing had unfastened in the night. He was taking in the view of the tops of my round breasts. Without even thinking, I leaned back a touch so that he could get a better look.

His eyes narrowed with a saucy glance. "Lassie, I'll

admire you every chance I get, don't you worry. But right now I'm going to go check the ship's position. I'll turn away so that you can dress quickly and I'll button you up."

I jumped out of bed, pulling on my dress, but not bothering with the petticoats. They were cumbersome, and I didn't know what would be required of me today. "Okay, I'm ready." He turned back, grinning when he saw I was wearing only the dress. "Much better," he said as he buttoned me up quickly. "This is not the place for fancy ladies. We might have to get you some true sailor's togs."

I nodded, feeling a light tap on my shoulder. "Done. You get down to the galley and help McGee with the food, alright?"

"Yes, sir," I said, darting out the door. As I carefully made my way through the dimly lit hallway, I found myself grinning. This would be my first full day on the ship, and I'd actually begin working to earn my keep.

It was all so exciting I felt like my heart might burst.

***

~ Chapter 6 ~ The Captain ~

** Breakfast **

"Larry, a word if ye will," I called across the deck.

My first mate trotted over, always quick for such a big man. "Aye, Cap'n?"

"I just wanted to see how you thought Flora was doing so far. Speak freely, you cannot offend me."

Larry grinned, turning his weathered face from severe to friendly. "I think she's a fine girl, Captain. We spoke a bit, and she knows a lot about sewing. She's eager to teach me things as well. I like that she wants to learn history, and more about the ship."

"She's getting on with the other men?"

He nodded. "Aye. They're trying to mind their tongues when she's about, but she hasn't seemed offended by the saltier curses. I like that she offered to help with the dishes without being asked. Shc's a proper lady in some ways, but not too proud to get dirty."

I was clearly pleased. "Thanks, Larry. I appreciate you helping with her. It might be good having a woman on board to tidy us up a bit. We've been becoming a pretty coarse lot. Now that we're down to the crew who is looking for more respectable trading, it might be better for us to pull up our bootstraps."

Larry nodded, pondering. "That makes sense, I s'pose. You've never mentioned bringing a lady on board before though. If you don't mind my asking, Cap'n, why now?" He flashed a saucy grin, knowing he was the only crew member who could get away with saying, "Aside from the fact that she's exactly your type, of course."

I lifted the back of my hand, but he didn't flinch, knowing that I was merely teasing.

Then I shook my head in frustration. "He was selling his daughter to strangers, mate. If I had refused, can you imagine what some honorless ruffian would have done with her? She may have become the toy of all manner of rough men." My jaw clenched, beyond furious at what I'd seen last night. "There are wounds on her back where her father lashed her. Can you find what's left of the salve, and put it on for her?"

The larger man looked uncomfortable. "You want me to touch your lady?"

"Think of it like fixing a broken piece of the ship." I clapped my first mate on the back. "You'll be fine. See you in the galley."

I went back to the charts, and the books where O'Doule and I had planned out our next several voyages. I must admit, his method of knowing where we were going at least seven to ten trips in advance was helping us greatly.

Before, we were simply sailing about, going with the strongest winds, or our desires to visit a certain port where we enjoyed the restaurants. We'd overtake smaller ships easily, liberating them of valuables as we went.

Unlike other ragged crews, we saw no sense in causing harm. Once our ship met another, they were terrified. Then they saw the sizes of Larry and I, and their hands shot into the air in surrender. It was quick as a whip to get them to hand over their gold and goods, and be on their merry way with no injuries.

We never messed with the poor fishermen, or the working ships. In fact, several times we've pulled up alongside to share an ale or a tall tale. The fancy boats with their crews dressed in matching uniforms to impress their rich owners, who sailed around purely for pleasure – those were the targets. It was obvious that no matter how much they had on the boat, they had a hundred times that amount back in one of their many houses.

I had liberated the sack of twenty gold pieces from the owner of a brand new lily white boat that was obviously on its first voyage. As a sailor, I would have congratulated him on his maiden run. But the way he'd been screaming at his crew, treating them like trash when it was clear he had no idea what he was talking about. I shook my head at the memory. What a horrid man. I felt for the crewmen, who must have been desperate for work to sign up with such a rig.

Reviewing our lists, O'Doule had made notes in his tidy handwriting about the features of each town, so that we could keep them all straight. Our next port of call had a wonderful butcher, and a fabric store that Larry had said was well stocked.

With Flora here, I could treat each of the boys to a new shirt, and her to a new dress. I realized I was grinning down at the weathered book as I thought of her being able to make herself a dress of her very own. Something fit for her new life here without pointless ruffles that overwhelmed her small frame.

She seemed to be fitting in perfectly in every way. I adored that the girl tried so hard. She seemed eager to begin working. I'd seen many a lass who thought she should be pampered and lazy, simply because she was a woman.

Closing the book and carefully shutting off the lamps, I went down to the galley. I heard Flora's sweet laugh mixed in with the gruff rumbling chuckles of the other men. When I entered, I instantly noticed the eating and cooking area was cleaner than I'd ever seen it.

"What's this dirt in the eggs?" Teeth asked suspiciously, poking at his plate with a fork. In all my life I'd never seen such a fussy eater.

"It's a touch of black pepper. Try it," Flora said softly.

Teeth looked up to see me, and nodded before he placed a forkful of food into his mouth. He chewed cautiously, then his eyes lit up. "Miss, this is golden!"

My gaze locked on her lovely features as she smiled softly.

She was proud. It looked good on her.

She bustled about, setting up a plate for me, and Davy as he arrived. "I don't mean to change your usual food," she said softly. "I just cook a certain way. If anyone doesn't like it, please tell me and I'll fix things any way you like."

Taking a bite of her scrambled eggs, my eyes rolled back in my head. "Lass, how the devil did you get these so…"

"Fluffy," Davy muttered with his mouth full. "And they taste huge."

Larry laughed. "How can taste have a size?" He took a bite, then cocked his side to the side, chewing and swallowing. "Davy, this might be the only time you hear it, so listen well. You're right. They taste huge."

Flora's bright laugh filled the room. "It's just a bit of pepper and oregano, and a touch of milk, then whipping makes them fluffy. Did you not do that before?"

McGee shook his head guiltily. "My Ma wasn't as sharp a cook as you, Miss. I'd have never thought of that."

I ate a few more bites, watching a flicker of sadness shimmer through Flora's eyes. "I wish I could have brought my cookbooks," she said softly. "And my pattern books. Had I known that I was leaving, I could have prepared better for you all."

Waving for her to come to me, I wrapped an arm around her waist as she stood close. "Don't feel guilty about something completely out of your control, my sweet girl." I wished I could kiss her sadness away, but it might frighten her. And not in front of the men. Instead, I gave her a little squeeze. "We're going to a town with a huge fabric store. You and Larry are going to go get the fabric to make each of the men a new shirt, and yourself a new dress."

Her pretty little mouth fell open for a second, and I had to lean away slightly to resist kissing her. She was far too tempting.

"Sir, I don't need–"

"We're pirates, we do as we like, remember?" I chuckled.

O'Doule shot me a look as he sat down to his plate after

Teeth left to mind the wheel. "You mean, traders. Shippers."

"Aye, that's what I meant," I chuckled. "Flora, would you like a new dress? You could make it fit comfortably for your new life of walking around on deck. You could make it more or less fancy, whatever you like."

Her lips turned up in the sweetest little smile. "I've never made myself a dress purely for comfort," she said softly. "I was always instructed to put myself on display to the local men to fetch a husband."

"Keep making food like this," Davy mumbled through his mouthful, "And we won't care if you have ten eyes and tentacles."

The men laughed uproariously. I nodded to her. "See? Now you'll have to ask each of the men what color shirt they'd like, and Larry will take stock of the things we need for the ship."

She nodded carefully. "Yes, sir. I'll see if I can haggle well and get good prices. I'll make the most of your money."

I shrugged. "It's the ship's money. Get a fair deal, and that's fine. These are good townspeople, and we want to be welcome in their port. Spreading a bit of the wealth is spreading the word that we're respectable."

I realized that Flora likely had no idea what we really did for work. She didn't ask, and that would likely come as she became more comfortable. Perhaps the details could wait through our transition from thieves to smugglers so that she respected us all a bit more.

Something rolled around the back of my mind, then came forward. "Flora, did you say that you can read?"

"Yes, sir."

She seemed surprised that a glance passed from man to man around the table, as they all grinned.

"So, if we gave you books and enough lamplight, you might read us stories in the evenings?"

"Of course, sir."

She rushed away to stir something on the stove, but she turned back to me. "Don't you all read? Did you not go to

                                   Haley Travis

school?"

The men all shrugged.

"O'Doule is the best reader among us," I said, "But his eyes get tired in the dark. He reads the notes and charts in the daylight, mostly." O'Doule nodded, eagerly eating his breakfast.

"I can read a fair bit," I said with only a touch of pride, "But I'm self-taught, mostly, so my reading is a bit slow for storytelling."

Davy jumped in. "Most of us were too busy trying to find work to go to schools, Miss."

Larry nodded. "I can read signs, most of the time. Not quick enough for tales."

Flora served us all another helping of fluffy eggs. "Then I'll go through whatever books you have, and find some stories you'd all enjoy."

"That's my lass."

Her eyes met mine, and I caught the sparkle. I know I should call her 'our lass', as she was a member of the crew. But it had slipped out. That way, she knew I meant it.

~ Chapter 7 ~ Flora ~

On the Open Sea

A great many things on this beautiful ship were wildly different. I was so accustomed to my quiet little life. I often didn't leave my house more than once or twice a week, beyond my daily five-minute walk to the edge of the forest and back. My mother insisted that I get a tiny bit of fresh air and sunshine on all clear days.

Although I'd always had mixed feelings about my mother, I wish that she could see me now. The air on the open sea was so unbelievably fresh and invigorating.

At breakfast, after the round of eggs to start them off, I thought the men's heads were going to explode when I suggested adding the tiniest pinch of cinnamon and brown sugar to the oatmeal. I made a sample batch so they could each try one spoonful. I was instantly declared the princess of all breakfast. Even Teeth loved it.

Accepting praise had always been difficult for me. I was so accustomed to my father's criticism that whenever someone said something nice, I couldn't trust it. But the men had nothing to gain by lying about my cooking, since they had to eat it.

I genuinely didn't think they had it in them to be dishonest to any member of the crew. It just wasn't their way to be anything but open.

After the washing up, I went to stand on the deck for a few minutes to get a face full of sun. I even rolled up my sleeves to feel the warmth on my arms.

"Hello, Miss," Larry said as he came up behind me. It was obvious that he was being very careful not to startle me.

"Hello. Can you believe the color of this sky?" I exclaimed.

He grinned, causing the corner of his eyes to crinkle. "Although I see it every day, Miss, sometimes it's still quite wondrous."

"I would never have believed that I could feel so open, puttering about on a ship full of..." I paused, I'm sure what to call the men.

"If you're thinking I might be offended by the word pirate, Miss, you're mistaken. Although if you were looking to be more polite, or the authorities were around, you could always say sailors. Or traders. Both of those are becoming more accurate with every voyage."

"Thank you," I said softly. I realized that he had to lean in to hear me sometimes.

"Miss, your voice is so soft. It's very ladylike, but out here with the constant wind, there will be times we need you to speak up a bit." He grinned. "Sometimes you'll even need to yell."

I shook my head. "I've never yelled in my life."

His laugh was more boisterous than I would have expected. "You're going to have to learn, Miss. It's important."

He pointed to where Davy was at the stern. He was on his knees with his ear to a barrel, rapping his knuckles down the wood until he made a face, then marked a line with a piece of charcoal.

"What if you needed to get his attention right now?" Larry asked. "Let's see if you could yell that far."

In all my years, I was taught that a lady never raises her voice. Not in anger, not ever. The thought of it was completely crass. Women should be seen and not heard. Yet Larry was right. If there was some occasion where I would have to get the men's attention, my weak little whispers would be useless.

Taking a deep breath, I called out, "Davy."

He moved on to another barrel, tapping and marking as he

went.

"Pretend you're a wild animal, Miss," Larry chuckled. "Or pretend there was a prize if you succeeded."

I looked up at him and tried to scowl, but it just made me giggle.

I tried to think about using my muscles to make my voice bigger. The power of my lungs. The power of my throat. Surely I could holler one word across such a distance.

"Davy!" I hollered at the top of my voice. He didn't even flinch, simply continuing his work.

O'Doule came up beside us. "Shall I holler for you, lass?" he asked.

"No, thanks," Larry explained. "I was trying to teach Miss Flora that she'll need to learn to raise her voice sometimes."

O'Doule nodded, taking off his spectacles to rub them on his shirt. "Aye. Lass, there will be times when you need to stop being a proper young lady, and remember that you're a crew member now. The rules of polite society do not apply out here."

I smiled at him. "Yes, thank you. I'll keep trying."

"Practice makes perfect," he said, nodding. "But you know, Davy's right ear is the one pointed at us, and that's the one that's half deaf."

O'Doule went down below, as I turned to look at Larry with my fists on my hips. He held up his hands as if I were going to slap him. "Miss, you know I meant for the best."

I burst into laughter, but this time, I didn't hold myself back. My parents weren't here to judge me. There were no open windows so the neighbors might hear. The ship was completely open to everything. I laughed louder than I ever had before, and it felt positively glorious.

Larry laughed with me for a moment, then grew serious. "Miss, I should mention this before I forget. I'm to help you with a problem on your back, I believe."

I closed my eyes and took a breath. "Yes. Thank you."

I followed him down to the pantry, and he rummaged around until he found a large metal tin. Since there was no one else in the galley at the moment, he led me to sit on a barrel.

"If you'll pardon me, Miss, I need to…"

I turned back over my shoulder to see the huge man practically sweating from nervousness. "It's all right, Larry," I said with a soft smile. "I'm sorry I can't reach the buttons myself."

I watched as he closed his eyes, swallowing hard, then giving his head a shake. As his eyes snapped open, he seemed completely focused on his task. He unbuttoned the back of my dress slowly, his thick fingers obviously giving him trouble. As he opened the panels of fabric, I felt him become still as a stone for a moment.

"Miss… I am so very sorry."

"I'm fine, but thank you."

I flinched as he began to rub the salve along one of the welts. "It doesn't hurt that much," I said quickly. "It's just chilly."

He worked quickly, coating the marks in a thin layer of ointment. He re-fastened the buttons part way up, then stopped. "Miss, if I left the top two buttons undone, your dress wouldn't be pressing against the sore areas as tightly. That might help it heal faster."

"Oh," I said. "That's a good idea." I turned to him. "I assume the men of the ship won't be scandalized if they see an extra inch of my back, will they?"

He smiled, putting away the tin and wiping his hands. "Not in the slightest, Miss. I'll never tell the tales of what some of us have seen."

"I probably don't want to know."

"You surely don't," he agreed as I jumped off the barrel. "Shall we go to the sewing area now?"

As soon as we set to work, I was thrilled that I was given the task mending sails with Larry. It was quite straightforward stitching, but obviously sails were much larger than any dress or sheet I had ever worked on. Having something I understood and felt confident about would help me feel more settled here.

"How are you getting along on the ship, Miss Flora?" he asked.

"Pretty well, I think," I said. "Everyone has been very patient with me."

His crooked smile was warm and genuine. "Miss, it takes everyone a little time to get their sea legs. Heck, it takes some people days just to figure out how not to trip on the ropes on deck. I think you're doing very well so far."

Watching him grin, I'd been wondering how honest and open I should be with him.

"Is there anything troubling you, Miss? I would be happy to help with anything I can."

I took a breath, collecting my thoughts and trying to put them in order. "The only thing that is truly strange to me is that my father basically owned me before, and now the Captain owns me. But he is a complete stranger. It's a bit… unsettling to think about."

Larry reached out to give my hand a little pat, surprising both of us. "Miss, do you think that the Captain treats me as if he owns me?"

"Not at all. You are a member of the crew, and he is obviously the leader. But it's all one big team here isn't it?"

"Five years ago the Captain won me in a game of cards," he said matter of factly. I must have looked astonished, as he laughed uproariously. "'Tis true, I swear, Miss. My previous Captain was paring down his crew, and we had never seen eye to eye." He looked uncomfortable for a second. "And I don't mean that as an insult, seeing as he only had the one eye."

"I know what you mean. But he actually risked you in a game of cards?" I shook my head. "That's just… Disrespectful."

"Aye, 'twas the best thing that ever happened to me," he nodded with a gentle smile, his hands still busy stitching. "Captain Samuels had given me a look first. He asked my permission with the raise of his eyebrow, waiting for my nod before he raised the bet."

I smiled to myself. That certainly sounded like the Captain

I was getting to know.

"Our Captain truly cares for his crew, Miss, and listens to those who have something to say. It is a wise man who takes advice from all who are brave enough to give it."

"And you don't feel like his possession?" I asked.

"Not at all. I know that if I truly wanted to leave, the Captain would shake my hand and send me on my way. He has never treated me differently than the other men here. I think he wanted to win me because he saw how strong I was, without being ill-tempered."

I grinned up at him. "Well, I am very glad that the Captain was dealt a good hand."

Larry suddenly glanced to make sure no one was around the doorway. Then he leaned in, lowering his voice to a whisper. "Miss, please never repeat this. The Captain is a very honorable man, and as honest as the day is long, except for the thievin' we sometimes need to do. But once a while, only in cards…" He winked. "The man cheats."

My laugh rang out, bouncing around the small wooden room, making Larry laugh as well.

Then he held out a bit of corner fabric. "Miss Flora, forgive me, but could you fix the point? It takes ten times as long with my thick fingers as it would with your dainty wee hands."

"Gladly," I said. The feeling of satisfaction of being a member of the crew, and truly contributing to the running of the ship, filled my heart with joy I could never have imagined. I'd always felt like my life was one long struggle against my father. Now I was part of a crew, and we were all headed in the same direction, even if I didn't know yet where that was.

It was a great relief to know that the Captain didn't take the ownership of people as seriously as I had feared.

I didn't even notice how many hours had passed, until I heard a few pans rattle. "Should I stay here and keep sewing, or help McGee with dinner?" I asked Larry.

He had been stitching away in his own little world for a spell. Looking up, he looked at how much of the sail I had edged since we began. "Good grief, Miss Flora. You're unbelievably quick. Sure, leave me to finish up here, and go give McGee a hand."

"Thanks," I said, quickly putting my needles and pins away before rushing into the galley area.

"How may I help?" I asked.

McGee turned with a grin. He seemed quite a good-natured fellow, although a bit quieter than the rest. "Thank you, Miss. I don't mean to give you the dirty work, but if you don't mind scrubbing up those potatoes and carrots."

"Good food is never dirty work," I smiled, pushing up my sleeves and grabbing the brush.

In about an hour, dinner was ready, and I helped fill up the plates, setting them around the table.

I noticed that Davy arrived first, fetching the tin mugs, and pouring out a round of ale from the keg in the corner. Then he turned to me. "Miss, would you like ale or water?"

"Oh. Um, I've never tried ale."

He poured a small sip into an empty mug and handed it to me. Swallowing carefully, I probably made a face as if I'd sucked a lemon. I heard Teeth laughing as he caught my expression on his way in. It tasted like old bread that had gone strange. "Water for me, thank you."

Davy laughed, rinsing the mug and filling it with water. "Don't you fear, lassie," he said, "It tastes bitter at first. Then you just drink more until you no longer care!"

I giggled, finding spoons, then sitting on a barrel. The rest of the men left the one beside me empty for the Captain. As I saw him come through the door, I felt a blush across my cheeks as I realized he looked for me first. His eyes softened the second he saw me, and he sat down very close.

"Lass, Larry tells me you're quick as a whip with sail edging. Well done."

He patted my hand where it rested on my leg, then he held it for a moment under the table, out of sight of the other men. For just a second, he entwined his fingers with mine, giving a squeeze before releasing me.

I was feeling all sorts of wild new things, but the deep ache in my belly was insistent. I needed to kiss him. Needed him to hold me. For the first time in my life, I realized that I needed… even more. And not for the man's pleasure, like I'd always been taught. For my own.

~ Chapter 8 ~ The Captain ~

** Sleep **

It was very reassuring coming down the galley to see dinner served, and Flora joking with the boys. Perhaps it was wrong to steal a little hand-holding under the table, but I couldn't resist. Her sweet blush drove me wild.

We enjoyed our meal, with the boys discussing what color shirts they should have, and O'Doule commenting on the upcoming weather patterns.

Flora seemed entranced, as if she were absorbing every bit of information like a sponge. When we were finished, Davy poured another round of ale, but I waved him away. Although I'd never admit it, I wanted to be alone with the little lass.

Once again, I nodded to the doorway, and she followed me. But this time she seemed more excited than nervous. Or perhaps I was just hopeful.

Reading women was a lot harder than knowing what men were thinking. With men, you could ask them straight out. If they weren't honest in their reply, that was their fault.

But women, especially a dear lass like Flora, seemed to have been taught to serve. They never thought to put themselves first. I hoped to break her of this habit someday. First, she'd have to become comfortable with me.

As soon as I shut the door, I spun her slim shoulders, unfastening the buttons at the back of her dress. "I see you're not quite buttoned up," I chuckled.

"Oh, Larry thought maybe leaving my dress loose would help my back to heal." She looked back at me over her shoulder with those sweet blue eyes.

"That's a good idea," I said, opening the back of her dress. I couldn't resist running my hands along her lower back for just a moment. She made a soft sigh, leaning toward me slightly.

It thrilled me that she enjoyed my touch. It was such a simple comfort, and I wanted her to learn to relax and let herself go.

I turned away as she changed into her nightdress. Once she was in bed, I pulled my clothing off, noticing as I slid in beside her that she'd left the top button open on purpose this time.

"What have you learned about the ship today?" I asked. I laid on my back, turned a bit toward her. She laid on her side with her arm curled under her head, facing me.

"I think I learned where most of the things in the kitchen are. I know where all of the sewing supplies are, and Larry had me edging a sail. I'm still learning the nautical names for things, but nobody seems to mind when I use the wrong terms."

"That's my lass," I smiled at her. I loved the beauty of her eyes when they twinkled with pride. "You just keep at it, and go at your own speed."

I watched as her eyes wandered from my lips to my tanned chest. I wish I knew if she was feeling the same strange pressure in her belly as I was. Reaching out, I dragged my thumb across her bottom lip, making her smile. Flora shifted again, her leg stretching out, accidentally brushing mine. Then she gasped as she realized I wasn't wearing pants tonight. They were too stiff and warm, and it was awkward to sleep in them.

She snapped her eyes up to mine, nearly shaking.

"Lass, there's something you're going to learn while you're out here at sea."

"Yes?"

"We live in our own world. There are no proper people to judge us. No village elders to give us orders. No fishwives to gossip. If we want something, we take it. If we think something will give us pleasure, we do it. No second thoughts. We sometimes leap without looking. Do you understand what I mean?"

"Um..."

"What I'm saying is, you can say anything you want. Do what you like. And if you want to touch me, go ahead."

Her tiny gasp amused me, but something in her eyes shifted. She cautiously reached out her hand, placing it over my heart. Stroking gently across the planes of muscle, my skin felt rough under her feminine hand.

"That feels nice," I said encouragingly. I reached out to cup her cheek. "You're even lovelier by lamplight."

"I can't get used to you being so sweet with me," she whispered.

I nodded. "You're used to men being rough and demanding, aren't you?"

"Yes."

"Any men besides your father?"

"Yes."

My jaw clenched, and couldn't help the wave of jealousy that flashed through me. "Who?"

"Thomas Glazenby. He was a shopkeeper in my village that my father had talked into marrying me."

"What happened?" My hand slid from her cheek to cradle the back of her head gently.

"He was a dreadful, nasty old man who spat when he spoke. He called me a trollop, and said he'd keep me..." She stopped.

"Go ahead."

She frowned before finally whispering, "On my knees, sir."

"Son of a bitch," I muttered under his breath. "Sorry, lass." I took a moment and a breath to compose himself. "Did he ever touch you?"

She shook her head emphatically. "No, sir. When my father insisted he court me, I tried to allow him to hold my hand, but couldn't continue."

"Good girl." I was surprised at the wave of relief I felt. Flora was so sweet that I wanted to think of her as pure. At the very least, not having been taken unless she desired it.

"My father said that by refusing to wed him, I disgraced us all. That's when he started rationing my food even more, and saying that I was eating him out of house and home. When I didn't change my mind after a month, that's when he tried to beat the evil out of me."

I tucked my arm under her shoulders, drawing her to me so that she was snuggled against my chest as she had been this morning. She smiled up at me and resumed wandering her hand across my skin. She stroked upward to my shoulder, then along the length of my arm.

"Where did you get all of these tattoos?" she asked.

"In many ports, across many countries," I said with a touch of pride.

"Some of these are lovely drawings." She pointed to a scene of a dragon over a mountain on my right bicep. "I've seen the woodcut this is taken from in a book."

"You have a sharp recollection, lass. You must have done well with your schooling."

"Of course, sir. My mother was a teacher before she married."

"I like a clever lass. Sometime soon, we'll have some ale and you can read us a real story instead of our own tales we've heard a hundred times before." She was finally relaxed against me, tucked right into my side. "I knew that you'd find ways to improve this ship," I joked.

Her eyes sparkled as she grinned. "I promise not to start decorating, and adding floral fabrics in every corner."

I leaned down to kiss her forehead lightly. "You decorate the world just by being in it."

The blush on her fair cheeks was so fetching I could barely control myself. I shifted, holding her so that she could either cuddle against me, or roll away. I was delighted that she used me for warmth, her tender body so soft against my hard frame.

I kissed her forehead again, and murmured, "Goodnight, lass."

Examining her eyes, I wondered if a chaste kiss would leave her wanting. It certainly left me needing more. As I leaned down toward those soft lips, it warmed my heart that she stretched up to meet me.

This time, my arm held her closer. Her little hand gripped me tightly as she pulled in. The blissful heat overtook us for a moment, her mouth opening slightly as she made the sweetest faint sigh.

I reluctantly leaned back, not wanting to overwhelm her. Then I kissed the tip of her nose, making her giggle. "Sweet dreams," I said, holding her against me as we drifted off.

***

I awoke to find that we had both shifted in the night. My arms were wrapped completely around her, and our legs were entwined. Her silky thigh lay bare over mine in a manner that was quite indecent. Yet I couldn't bring myself to pull away, my heart racing wildly.

Looking down into her eyes that were just beginning to open, I tried to keep my breathing steady. Her hand wandered over my chest again, and I tilted my chin toward her instinctively.

The urge to kiss her traveled through me, igniting every nerve. But I'd already taken too many little moments, without quite being sure what she wanted.

"You said the sea is a place of freedom, right?" she whispered.

"Aye, lass. We take what we like."

I held still as a stone while she seemed to think for a spell.

The questions all melted away as she stretched up, pressing her lips against mine. My arms gripped her tighter, pulling her up toward me as her lips parted. She melted against me, our skin pressed together. I nibbled her bottom lip, and she almost giggled, but then I grabbed her, lifting her to lie on top of me.

Her soft gasp aroused me more, and her tongue instinctively darted between my lips. My hands caressed her lower back, gliding down to cup her behind in a very familiar way. Flora froze, perhaps realizing that she was practically squirming on top of me. My excitement became evident, pressing up against her knickers.

But she didn't stop. The feeling of her body pressed against me was exhilarating. Our lips parted more, and my tongue darted into her sweet mouth. Her hands wrapped into the back of my hair, and her legs spread as my thickness pressed between them.

My eyes flew open as she seemed to lose herself in the moment. I finally broke off the kiss, but continued stroking her tight little backside. "Lassie, I had no idea you were so frisky in the mornings."

"I... I'm sorry, sir." She tried to roll away, but I held her in an iron grip. Shockingly, instead of being afraid of being at my mercy, her eyes filled with lust. I released her immediately, and was relieved that she stayed in place.

"Stay a moment, lass. You feel so lovely pressed against me." She searched my eyes, then paused. "Whatever you're thinking, sweet girl, go ahead."

Slowly she leaned down, setting her lips at the hollow of my throat, kissing me roughly, fluttering her tongue over my skin. She moved downward, using both of her hands and her lips to massage my chest.

A soft moan rumbled from deep within me, and I hope it thrilled her to know how much she aroused me. I was gently rocking her against me, and my manhood was now pressing firmly into her stomach. I felt a shudder run through her, and immediately rolled her to the side. "Sorry, lass, I didn't mean to frighten you."

"You didn't..."

I placed a finger over her lips, then removed it and gave her a small kiss. I looked out the small window, checking the angle of the sun. "We've overslept. The boys will likely tease us at breakfast. Dress quickly now."

She jumped up and turned her back to me to remove the nightshirt. As she pulled her dress on, Flora said, "I think that salve helped a little already."

"Good to hear," I said, sneaking a glance. Her slim legs that had been wrapped around me moments before were in view for a second before she pulled her dress down. But those lash marks, still clearly visible if perhaps a bit less red and angry, made my heart lurch with sorrow.

I should not be touching her so freely. Even though I was extremely relieved that she kissed me of her own accord, I needed to be careful with my timid lass. She should be touched with nothing but the most tender hand.

"Don't forget to have Larry put on more of that salve. You should do that every day."

"Yes, sir."

I knew I should have her call me by my name eventually. But dammit, it excited me to the very core every time she called me 'sir'.

***

~ Chapter 9 ~ Flora ~

** Storm **

It was lovely that I was already learning the routine of the ship. First, there was breakfast with the men, filled with laughter and good-natured ribbing. Then most of them went to different spots to work on repairs, toolmaking, rope making, and the like.

Larry seemed much less embarrassed as he spread ointment across my back, then he set me up with the day's sewing before he left to repair rigging. It was nice that he checked in with me every few hours. Somehow, sewing all day long wasn't nearly as exhausting as my days back at home. Perhaps it was the fresh air. More likely, it was the way I was complimented on how much I'd accomplished, instead of belittled.

I was delighted that everyone seemed to truly appreciate the dinner I helped with. Even Teeth enjoyed my potato and carrot mash with rosemary.

After McGee and I washed up the dishes, I had a book selected to read to the men. Yet when Davy gathered a few of the lamps together, I realized my knees were beginning to tighten up. The floor was swaying gently.

O'Doule turned to the Captain, who gave a nod. "The storm swung south much faster than we thought. Davy, put out the lamps. Flora, stay with Larry," the Captain commanded.

As most of the lights went out and the men all bolted for the deck, Larry took my hand and helped me navigate the swaying steps.

                    Haley Travis

"Don't be scared, Miss," he said, flashing me his warm smile even in the near dark. "We are perfectly safe. Just come up for a moment and I'll show you how to watch the sky properly."

There were no stars to be seen. The sky was a menacing rolling blanket of deep black and gray clouds. A few last blue streaks showed the sunset to the west, but from the north, the winds were blowing briskly.

Larry pointed to where it looked like the edge of the sea had become blurry. "That's the line of rain," he said. "If we had any land in view, we could calculate how long it would be before we got there. But without a reference point, all we can say is that it's coming soon."

The waves were becoming choppier, and I had to see them for myself. Clutching the railing, I held tight to look down at the waves that were now topped with frothy white peaks.

The wind seemed to take three seconds to turn from a stiff breeze to an outright gale. Before I could even pull in enough breath to squeal, the clouds released. The rain hit us in sheets. It didn't seem like it was falling, more like it was being fired at us from a canon. It was freezing. My bones began to shake before I even fully realized that I was wet.

Larry's strong arm gripped my waist almost roughly, hauling me down below decks.

Before I could even wipe the frigid water from my eyes, he had me wrapped in a blanket, sitting on the Captain's bed. "Promise me you'll stay right here," he said urgently.

"Yes, of course."

Even over the roar of the rain, I heard the Captain bellow, "Where is–"

"She's safe in your quarters, sir," Larry hollered.

Then all I heard was a blur of voices yelling back and forth to each other as they lashed down a few stray barrels, quickly changing course.

I couldn't tell how much time had passed, as the room was nearly pitch black. I was shaking, afraid to try to take off my wet things when I couldn't see. The chill began to wear through me, and my bones felt brittle.

After what seemed like a long time, the swaying of the ship settled back to a gentle roll. Not too long after, the door opened and the Captain came in with a lamp. "My sweet girl, we're anchored in an inlet for the night. Everything's fine."

"Ok-kay."

"You've survived your first storm, my lassie." The way he called me his warmed my heart, though the rest of me was so chilled I couldn't feel my feet.

"Lass, is that your teeth chattering?"

"Yeth," I muttered, trying to stand up to get out of my cold, wet clothing now that I could see.

As soon as the Captain saw that I was wet, he took over. Ripping everything off of me, he threw me naked into the bed, ignoring my shocked gasp. He turned the lamp up high, and lit another. Then he tore his own clothing off, getting under the blankets with me.

"Now is not the time for shame," he said. He turned me away from him so that my entire back was pressed against his wide chest, his strong legs up against mine. His arms curled around me so that his hands were flat against my stomach, pulling me tight. "Skin on skin is the fastest way to warm you through."

"I bet-t-t you're g-g-glad it's me that's frozen, and not-t-t Larry," I chattered, with a little giggle.

"You have no idea," he said with a snort

It didn't take long for me to warm up, and soon the quaking stopped. But the feeling of being naked in his arms was starting a different sort of trembling. His hands parted. Slowly the right slid up to my breast, as the left glided down to rest against the mound between my legs.

Gently running his fingers through my short curls, he asked, "Lassie, are you warm?"

"Yes," I breathed.

"Should I let you go now?"

"No."

His hand cupped the soft skin of my breast, squeezing

gently, traveling lazily around in a circle as my head tipped back against his shoulder.

I'd never experienced such raw feelings, as if my body had completely taken over and my normally fretful mind had washed overboard.

His other hand slowly moved lower, taking hold of my right thigh and pulling it upward. Then he pushed down the left so that my legs were spread, my feminine parts open. His fingertips wandered along my inner thigh. The butterflies I usually felt in my stomach when he kissed me were now much lower.

Hearing myself moan softly surprised us both. My skin felt like it was on fire everywhere he touched me.

His thick dark voice murmured, "Shall I stop, lassie?"

"No. Please..." I arched over my left shoulder to kiss him, as his hand possessed the space between my thighs.

His fingertips cautiously swept through the soft curls, dragging along the tender folds of my most delicate skin. As he gently stroked me, I felt things simmering deep inside, as if everything were tightening.

The need for him to touch me came from a place so deep inside I'd never known it was there. A part of me was waking up. A yearning so intense that it nearly frightened me.

The way his lips hungrily captured mine sent shivers through my spine. I couldn't stop moaning and gasping into his mouth. His fingers found my sensitive passage, and he slowly, gently slid inside. I was surprised at the sensation of wetness, and found that it somehow aroused me even more that my body was taking over.

There was a feeling of fullness as he entered me with one finger, moving in and out. His rough hand brushed against my softness, making my breath hitch as my heart raced. Bringing his thumb to the bit of skin just above the opening, he swirled against it, sending sparks straight through me. My belly tightened and everything felt strangely raw.

Having him possess my body in this manner was enchanting, as he controlled me completely. The heat inside me grew until I was burning, tense, feeling like I was about to fall over a ledge.

"Oh, what..." I tried to ask, the trembling beginning in my core and hips at the same time.

"Let go, precious. Come for me." His dark command washed through me, as his fingers worked deeper and faster. Suddenly I was falling, explosions behind my eyes as I squealed in bliss.

"Oh, oh..." I cried, gasping for air as I shook in his arms.

When my trembling stopped, I rolled over to face him. I felt half-crazed. He seemed both proud and delighted. "You sounded like you enjoyed that, lass."

I nodded, euphoric and dumbfounded. "Oh my," I managed.

He pulled me closer, and I could plainly feel how much my arousal had affected him. Somehow, that made me feel even more excited. Taking a deep breath, I moved the hand that had been pressed against his chest, and slid it down. I moved past the taut ripples of his stomach to feel the thick shaft of his manhood.

My hand fluttered along his skin, which was softer, sleeker than I had expected. It felt a bit like a rod of iron wrapped in silk. As I worked my way downward, I became worried as my hand went farther and farther. I would never have thought it would be that big.

The more my hand ran along the surface, the more the Captain's eyes softened. He wasn't relaxing, it was as if he were partially in a dream.

"Do you like this?" I asked, unsure.

"Yes, lass," he said gently. "But what if you used both hands?"

I sat up, wrapping both hands around his shaft. Now that I could actually see it, I was intrigued. There seemed to be a layer of skin that moved over the tip strangely. He reached down, and showed me how to pull it back, then run my palm across the top.

It was like playing a strange game, as I listened to his

breathing. When I slowed down, he seemed dreamy. When I sped up, or increased the pressure, his breathing quickened. I was delighted that he appeared to be enjoying my touch so thoroughly, and I tried increasing the pressure and the speed at the same time.

His low moan surprised and delighted me. "Yes, lass, keep doing that." I grinned up at him to see his dark eyes tense. Having his huge body under my control was a strangely intoxicating power.

It didn't feel dirty or wrong in the slightest. It felt like I was bringing him the greatest pleasure, which thrilled me to pieces. I stroked faster, feeling his shaft throbbing in my fingers.

His muscles clenched, and his dark eyes were burning into mine. When I looked down, I felt his organ shudder in my hands, then pump thick bursts of white cream across his chest, while he groaned, clutching the back of my hair.

He lay still for a moment, blinking, as his breathing returned to normal. I waited patiently until he spoke. "That was lovely, my sweet girl."

"Did I do a good job?"

He chuckled. "The best." Grabbing a rag from behind the head of his bed, he wiped off his stomach, then turned back to kiss me.

I wrapped my hands around his shoulders, but it wasn't enough. Rolling on top of him, I instinctively found myself straddling him, legs wide, but this time there were no knickers between us. Feeling the urges of my body take over, I pressed the end of his shaft between my legs, nestling him inside my little folds of skin.

It felt so natural, so right. Grabbing my behind he moved with me, beginning to push the tip of his shaft into my tunnel, then his eyes grew wide. He shifted me back to the side, rolling me away. "Lassie, we can't."

"Why not?" I whispered, terrified that I'd displeased him somehow.

"At least, not tonight," he said gently. "You've had a chill and a fright, and we've explored enough for now."

I nodded, trying not to feel rejected. At least he'd finally touched me in that way, which proved that he did indeed want me. That was a great relief. I'd never felt so drawn to a man before, and the thought of him not wanting me was horrific.

He must have seen the confusion in my eyes.

"Lassie," he nearly growled, "Don't you dare think I don't want you. I've never desired a woman this much in my life. We just need to take some time. Can you trust me?"

I nodded. Then he kissed me until I was nearly dizzy before tucking us in to sleep.

***

~ Chapter 10 ~ The Captain ~

* Paperwork *

I was grateful to have O'Doule on board to take care of the paperwork and sums. Although I was fairly accurate at scheduling and keeping the accounts straight, it was an annoying task. It gave me a bit of a headache just to think about.

I enjoyed the planning, the plotting, and deciding on the routes. I seemed to have a knack for keeping large amounts of information in my mind at once so I could pick and choose the best routes for what we needed.

It was a great relief that this group of men agreed we should do less outright thieving, and more smuggling and trading. Since we certainly appeared like a scurvy band of pirates, local authorities in small towns wanted nothing to do with us.

This made it extremely simple for rum running, and quick shipments of slightly illegal supplies such as various pistols that would otherwise take far too long to procure through official channels.

We also happened to meet a few rigs who were running exotic spices up from the south. Just because they were undocumented didn't make them any less delicious. It was extremely lucrative. Since spices were only classified if people had heard of them, it also wasn't quite illegal, technically.

Once people had seen us travel by the port several times, they entrusted us to run regular goods from town to town as well. Loads of grain, seed and farming supplies, and hand-knit sweaters were not the most exciting cargo, but it was fair money.

Although we didn't want to get into the habit, we even ran a young man back to his hometown a few months ago, so that he would arrive in time for his sister's wedding.

I never told the boys I barely charged him for the passage, just the equivalent of regular room and board. O'Doule had given me that fatherly smile and nod at the time, understanding. Since we were passing through anyway, best that the young lad save his bits of silver to fetch his sister a nice gift.

It was still best that we avoided the authorities as much as possible. But since we weren't flying the black, and we did have legal cargo aboard, I was reasonably certain that we would pass inspection.

Still, with Teeth and Davy and their sharp eyes on watch as much as possible, we simply avoided all large ships. The Fortune's Favor was extremely fast and very maneuverable. This gave us the ability to blink out of sight quickly.

I would never have kept Flora with us if I thought she'd be in danger. A few years ago, when the outfit was quite dishonorable and often chased by men with bayonets, I would have dropped her off in the nearest town where we had some acquaintances to care for her.

Now, I was fairly certain that she was safe with us. If we were arrested, we would say she had simply purchased passage to a nearby port, and beg the authorities to take her there safely.

Which reminded me that I'd have to speak with Flora about learning how to act. All of the boys were able to turn into a character when need be. It was astounding how Davy could suddenly look like a boy small enough to be still in britches. Or McGee could instantly become the drunken uncle that we were all caring for on our way back from the pub.

Part of our shady life was learning how to get through awkward moments. I never planned to put Flora in that position, but I should attempt to prepare her in case the occasion cropped up.

I was glad that the wee lass was finally going to be able to visit another town. Long ago, I vaguely recalled how exciting it was the first time I explored an entirely new village. There was nothing terribly different, but every single thing was just a tiny bit new. Everything seemed fresh and more interesting.

It was extremely disappointing that I was unable to accompany Flora on her first little expedition, but I'd send Larry to watch over her. They seemed to get on quite well, and there was nobody I could trust her with more.

***

~ Chapter 11 ~ Flora ~

Shopping in Parrinport

That afternoon, while I attended to the pile of sewing projects, I found myself distracted. I stabbed my finger a few times with the needle as my mind wandered away, and I found myself unable to focus.

After that amazing night with the Captain, I felt closer to him than ever before. Yet I was confused as to why he wouldn't take me completely. I didn't know much about the ways of men. From what I had gleaned back in my village, it was all that most men wanted from women besides a good meal.

Years ago, my mother had awkwardly told me about "the snake in the cave", and I'd listened with rapt attention.

"But how does it work?" I had asked, the curiosity overtaking me even more than my embarrassment.

"Just let the man do as he will, and try not to fight back," mother had said.

"Is there only one way?"

Mother's lips tightened, and her hand had fluttered to a tiny scar on the side of her left jaw. "Sometimes he might try to get you to put his manhood into your mouth like a common whore." She stroked the inch of disturbed flesh without even thinking. "Sometimes it's worth fighting back, and sometimes it isn't."

The memory had always upset me terribly. But now that there was an actual man in my life, the conversation took on more meaning. The thought of pleasing the Captain thrilled me on a level I didn't even understand. I wanted him to want me. I wanted to satisfy his every need. Yet I could barely get my hands around his… piece. The thought of it sliding between my lips... looking up at him while he smiled his encouragement...

I dropped the sewing needle, grabbing it just before it disappeared between the floorboards.

"Something wrong, Miss?" Larry inquired as he came into the room to check on me.

I felt my cheeks flush, which likely told him that my mind had wandered far from my task. "Sorry."

Larry nodded in understanding. "There are many things here that are very new to you, aren't there?"

"Yes."

"You seem to be handling it better than most. You've not even been seasick," he said with a touch of admiration.

"When I was small, I would sneak down to the docks and lie in an old boat at the end of the pier, where nobody could see me," I recalled dreamily. "It was my secret place to run away from the world. The rocking of the waves, the lilt of the water has always calmed me."

"Even the way you speak is pretty," Larry said.

"Thank you." I smiled at my new friend, realizing with delight that I was somehow closer with him already than I'd ever been with my school mates. "I'm glad that I'm here to share the work with you."

He laughed. "I had three main jobs on the Fortune. Lifting the heaviest cargo, sewing, and listening to the Captain when he needs an ear." His slightly lopsided grin amused me. "I'm very glad you're here to take care of the stitchin' now."

I giggled, then looked over at him as he sat with me for a moment. His face was quite rugged, and would have looked downright frightening if not for the warmth in his eyes and his easy smile. "Larry, may I ask you a question?"

"You want to know how I got this huge scar."

I nodded. "I guess everyone must ask you that. I'm sorry – you don't have to tell me."

"It's okay. I used to tell women that it happened while saving a puppy from a mountain lion, thinking they might find that endearing."

I snickered but quickly fell quiet. My curiosity about this gentle man had been growing, and this seemed like a tale that was important to him.

"I don't know that it's a very exciting story," he said softly. "My first Captain wasn't always as organized as Captain Samuels. He didn't always inform the crew of what was going on. This made it difficult for us to help each other out on our various…" He paused, looking up at me with a worried glance. "Excursions."

I reached out to pat his hand. "Larry, I can imagine that life is rough out here, and I'm sure that some jobs are a bit, shall we say, shady. Just skip over that part if it makes you feel better."

He nodded quickly. "Thank you, Miss. So, I was dropping off a small barrel of, um, special powder. Three of us had been carrying barrels, but I knew that mine had a very sensitive cargo.

"When we stashed them in the back of a stable as the Captain had instructed, I noticed that the other two crewmen decided to take a break, sitting on the barrels and lighting up a cigar."

His eyes grew tense. He didn't look up at me as his hands began to shake slightly from the memory that obviously made him uncomfortable. "I knew that cargo was supposed to be a secret, but I couldn't let the young lads take a chance on being blown to kingdom come. As I was deciding what to do, I saw one of them throw a match near the bottom of the special barrel, which looked like it had a small leak."

He looked up at me with an absolutely haunted expression. "Secrets be damned, Miss, I couldn't let anyone be maimed like that. I charged them, knocking them both through the back doorway of the stable just before the black powder went up."

"Oh my goodness," I whispered. "Thank goodness you noticed in time."

He shrugged. "Not in time to save the stable. It exploded, and we had to run for the docks as if the devil himself were at our heels. I didn't even realize until we reached the ship that a piece of flying wood had clipped my ear and half of my face."

"But that's the only place you were hurt?" I asked frantically.

"Aye. Well, I had a few bruises and scrapes on my back from other bits of wood, but that was nothing. The two younger lads were in front of me, so they were safe."

"And if the Captain had warned them that one piece of your cargo was dangerous, they would never have done such a thing?" I asked.

"Exactly, Miss."

I nodded, thinking. "Our Captain keeps everyone well informed, does he?"

Larry smiled, his eyes warm and relaxed again. "Aye, Miss. He might not tell us every detail, but he always lets us know the crux of what's going on, and warns us well if there is anything dangerous."

I nodded, staring down at my hands for a moment, thinking. It was one thing to consider the tales of pirate life from afar, but it was very different now that I was sitting on a ship.

"Miss, this ship doesn't carry much dangerous cargo anymore," he said quickly. "What little weaponry we do transport, it's only things that can be packaged safely. Captain Samuels doesn't take chances with things like black powder, especially after I told him what happened to me. It's only small barrels, and they're clearly marked. No secrets."

I smiled up at him. "Well, that's good to know."

"And he would never put you at risk, Miss. I hope that you know that. No matter what happens with the rest of us, he would do everything to keep you safe."

I couldn't help giggling. "What if there was a fortune to be made smuggling something impossibly illegal?"

"Then he would stash you at McGee's mother's house, or somewhere else perfectly safe while we made the run," he said quite seriously. "I'm just assuming, of course. He hasn't spoken to me about it. But I know that he would never take you into harm's way."

Looking out across the gently rolling sea, I realized that I felt safer with these men that I had in my own village. What a strange world.

Then I saw something on the horizon. "Larry, is that Parrinport?"

He turned his head to glance. "Aye." He glanced back to my stitching, then his head suddenly perked up. "Quick, come with me."

I dropped my sewing and tried to keep pace with the big man as he dashed to the forecastle. I gripped the railing beside him as we stood at the bow, the wind in our hair. Now that I could see the land coming toward us, I had a better sense of how fast the ship was going.

"I'll tell you a secret, Miss Flora," Larry grinned with nearly childlike glee. "No matter how many times a sailor has circled the world, it's always exciting to reach port."

The salty air was catching me full in the face, nearly taking my breath away, and giving me a bit of a chill. It was exhilarating. Refreshing. Like my soul was being cleansed, and every stress and needless thought was scrubbed away by the feeling of flying across the water.

By the time I could almost make out individual trees along the shore, the ship had slowed down, as Teeth and McGee dropped the sails.

Larry patted my shoulder, leaving me to chat with the Captain. It was hard not to nearly jump up and down in excitement as I rushed to scrub my face and comb my hair before we reached the shore.

It was brilliantly exciting for me to visit a completely new town for the first time. But I wasn't sure why the Captain sent Larry to accompany me instead of him. I didn't mean to overhear, but I heard them use the words "authorities" and "posters", yet wasn't sure what that meant.

Perhaps the Captain was thought to be dangerous around

these parts. It was amusing that I couldn't imagine him as fearsome, but knew he likely could be if the occasion presented itself. It certainly wasn't my place to ask. I felt that I should simply follow orders as best I could. It was also quite possible that the Captain simply had to stay with the ship to settle business dealings.

He gave me a little sack of money before we left. "Flora, you spend as much as you need to. This is your first port of call, so if you see a trinket that you'd like as a token, feel free."

His large hand cupped my cheek for a second, as the warmth of his gaze washed through me. "Stay with Larry and you'll be safe, lass."

Then he gave us both a nod, and Larry and I walked off the ship. When we stood on the dock, Larry held me by the elbow for a second, keeping us still. It felt downright funny to be on solid ground.

Larry smiled from under the wide brim of the hat he had donned for our excursion. "Just take a moment, Miss. Like when you come aboard, your legs need to get used to the swell of the sea. Now we need to get our land legs back."

After a pause, we walked down the dock and along the path toward the busiest part of the village. I instantly felt nervous, nearly tucking into Larry's side. I didn't know these people. Should I worry about what they might think of me? Or was that just my father's voice still in the back of my head?

"Miss, part of blending in is looking confident. Like you belong here. If you'll pardon my sayin', you look like you want to disappear into the pathway. Try standing tall with your chin up. Pretend that's a thousand gold pieces in your purse." He flashed a grin as I tried to arrange myself. "That's it."

It was the first time I'd ever seen Little Larry in a long-sleeved shirt. I almost asked him why, then realized it was to hide his tattoos. Normal villagers likely didn't take too kindly to frightening looking men, or long-distance sailors.

"Larry, is it Sunday?"

"I think it's Tuesday, Miss."

Looking around at the people on the cobblestone paths, the men were mostly in dark pants with white shirts, but a few of them had shirts of light blue and green. The women wore extravagant dresses in all manner of colors. I had assumed it must be Sunday best. Did people dress like this on weekdays? It seemed amazing.

Larry guided me around a corner, toward a large shop with a sign that read, "Gerrard's Fabrics and Notions."

"That must be it," I said. I'd never been to a new town before, but somehow visiting my favorite kind of store was very exciting.

"As you shop, Miss, I'll stay out of your way. But I can hold your purse, and carry everything for you."

"Okay."

"It's okay to let people think I'm your servant," he said softly.

"Why on earth would I do that?"

He shrugged. "People don't think much of seafaring folk, or strangers. I'm so big that if I'm quiet, most people assume I'm slow. It's okay to let them think that. It keeps them from being afraid."

As we walked into the store, my hand flew to my mouth to stifle my gasp. The shop was huge. The selection was incredible. I'd never dreamed of so many different kinds of fabric in one place. And the colors… my head was nearly swimming.

I walked around the shop in a slow circle, noting what colors the men wanted for their shirts. The Captain had told me to choose something for him. My eyes fell upon a dark, mysterious green fabric that would make him look even more tan, even more beautiful. The thought of dressing a man had never occurred to me before. The thought that he was my man, in a way, fluttered through me with a strange warm glow.

The shopkeeper was a sturdy older woman who was very efficient. She cut me lengths of every fabric I needed, and helped me assemble needles, thread, a new marking pencil, and other little notions I required.

"Is that everything, Miss?" she asked. She seemed quite pleased, as if this was a big sale for her.

"Almost. I'll just need a moment to double-check."

Larry had been standing silently near the door. "Miss, did you get fabric for a new dress for yourself?" he said softly.

"Oh, yes, thank you." I turned to examine a dark silvery gray fabric that would have been the nicest dress I'd ever had.

Looking to Larry, I pointed. "Is this appropriate?"

He shook his head, smiling softly. "Perhaps for an everyday dress." He pointed to a bolt of cloth in a brilliant sea blue. "I think that one might suit you better, Miss. You should definitely get material for at least two."

The thought of owning a bright blue dress, just for the amusement of having it, was something I couldn't even fully think through. It was as if the idea were a circle and my mind was a square. It wouldn't fit inside.

"Oh, yes," the shopkeeper gushed. "Blue is very stylish this season. Anything related to the sea and the water is very fashionable."

I heard a little gasp as she noticed my collar. My hand fluttered to my throat. I'd forgotten that in an attempt to look dressier, I'd made myself a collar of a black and blue velvet ribbon with a sea shell glued to the center.

"That's the most unusual necklace I've ever seen, Miss. Wherever did you get it?"

I smiled, but felt suddenly shy. "I made it, Ma'am."

"Where did you get that type of shell? I've never seen one in with peach streaks like that."

I stifled my giggle. There was a large bowl in the ship's sewing area filled with the prettiest stones and shells that the men had found throughout their many adventures. They'd said that I could help myself to anything.

"My friends travel a lot, Ma'am. They've explored many beaches, and kept a few pretty tokens."

"Have you ever made more?" she asked eagerly.

"I've never thought about it, Ma'am. I easily could."

"If you make more, please come to see me. I'll buy twenty

of them at twopence each."

I turned toward Larry. "How soon will we be back in Parrinport?"

"Likely in a few weeks, Miss."

"Thank you." I turned back to the shopkeeper. "I'm certain I could have twenty made for you then, with a variety of different shells. But I'd best buy a new roll of this velvet ribbon, please."

As we walked back to the ship with Larry carrying a pile of wrapped packages, I suddenly felt guilty. "Do you think the Captain would mind me spending his money on ribbon to make things for a shop? Should I have asked his permission first?"

Larry laughed, his rumbling chuckle making the dockworkers we passed laugh with him for no reason. "Aye, my pappy used to say 'tis best to ask forgiveness later than to ask permission in advance." He smiled down at me. "I'm sure it will be fine, Miss. Spending money on something you need isn't thievin'."

As we approached The Fortune's Favor, I looked up to see the Captain on deck. The way his expression lit up as he saw me thrilled me to bits.

He rushed down the plank to greet me, sweeping me up in a huge hug. His lips brushed my ear as he whispered, "I missed you, lass." Pulling away, he kissed my forehead so quickly I don't think anyone else noticed. "How did your shopping go?" he asked as he led me onto the ship.

"Wonderfully, sir." I saw that Larry was already carrying the parcels down to the sewing table. "I got everything we needed, but also some velvet ribbon." I pointed to my necklace. "The shopkeeper liked this so much that she asked me to make more for her to sell."

I watched his eyes carefully, hoping that I hadn't stepped past any rules.

"Brilliant," he grinned. Then he turned to call out to O'Doule. "Aren't we passing the wee beach at Sonderlee on our way to Grimmington?"

"Aye, Captain. Did you want to make a stop?"

"Yes. Just for a few hours. We'll pick up some fresh fruit, and we can all have a run on the beach."

"Aye," O'Doule nodded. "We could all use some time ashore."

The Captain led me to a bench on the deck, sitting me close beside him. "That shell you're wearing comes from Sonderlee, and we can go help you find more."

I was stunned that he'd make a special trip just for me. "Thank you, sir. I was planning to just use the bits from the little treasure bowl."

He shook his head, leaning in to examine my necklace. "I see the pink bits in the shell that I bet women like. This will be a fun excursion. We've never treasure hunted for shells before," he chuckled. Then he looked at me carefully. "What's wrong, lass?"

"I'm… I just… I'm surprised," I stammered. "I wouldn't think that anyone would go out of their way to help me sell some tiny bits of jewelry."

He took my hand in his. "Lass, out here we help each other. If you want to make things, we'll get you what you need." He nodded to where Teeth and McGee were loading barrels, lashing them to the deck with ropes. "We get plain bread when we can because Teeth's stomach can't stand the heavy grains. We sail to Laurel Point every June so that McGee can attend his mother's birthday dinner. We care for our ship, and that includes the people on it."

I squeezed his hand. "Thank you," I said softly, looking up into his deep eyes. I still couldn't quite believe how close I felt to a man I'd known for less than a week.

~ Chapter 12 ~ The Captain ~

* *Sonderlee Beach* *

It was hard to believe that the girl running across the sand with her skirts hitched up to her knees was the same timid little lass who had seemed so worried about being proper.

Her long blonde hair flew in the breeze as Davy chased her, threatening to drop a wee fish down the back of her dress. They were the youngest crew members, and it warmed my heart to see them carrying on like brother and sister.

Larry and O'Doule had gone a bit inland with giant baskets to fill with fruit. O'Doule knew all of the safe varieties and was brilliant at selecting fruit that was ready to eat today, and what would ripen over the coming weeks. Larry's long arms could easily reach everything we needed.

McGee had just returned with buckets from the stream a short walk inland, so we could stock up on fresh water. Before we left, we'd all carry a few buckets to lighten the load.

Flora, Davy, and Teeth had been collecting shells and stones, until two of them ran off. Flora's little squeals filled the air until she finally held up her hands in surrender. "Please," she begged, "I can't run anymore."

Davy waved the fish in front of her face until she shrieked, then tossed it back into the sea. The two of them got back to work where Teeth was sorting piles of shells.

It was admirable how intensely Teeth was taking his task. I strolled by to see he had found dozens of small shells in the appropriate size, and had them all sorted by styles and colors.

"Instead of traders, we'll soon be jewelry artists," I joked.

Teeth looked up at me in delight. "I've always thought about becoming a silversmith," he said. "My Uncle Rupert crafts things from silver. It's an interesting trade."

"I bet it is," I said. "Perhaps we can look into that someday."

O'Doule came back to the beach with a giant basket of fruit, and I rushed over to take it from him. He tried to protest, but I was much larger, and there was no shame in a man knowing his limits.

"You just hauled it all the way down the path, let me help," I said, taking the basket down to the rowboat. I joined him back on the beach, as we looked to the sunset, and the slight wispy clouds to the north.

"Should be fine sailing for several days, I think," he said.

"Good. We aren't in a hurry, but it's always best to get ahead of things. Impressing our new clients by having their shipments a bit early is likely a good thing."

"Aye, 'tis true," O'Doule agreed. Then he regarded me thoughtfully. "You know, Captain, having a fairly regular schedule from Crossly Port to Parrinport might help us in a few ways."

"How's that?"

"It would create a reasonably reliable schedule for transporting the raw goods, spices, and whatnot," he said. "But running Miss Flora to her ladies' shop every few weeks is a good, respectable task."

I nodded, stroking my slight scruff of beard thoughtfully. "You're right. I've noticed that a few of the traders would like to be apprised of the timelines. Running a sweet lass to the beach for supplies, and to the shops to sell her wares… That does sound wholesome indeed."

"Since we're no longer runnin' up the black flag, perhaps we can develop our new reputation around our dependability?" O'Doule suggested.

I couldn't help laughing. "Aye, that sounds fearsome indeed."

He shot me a flat stare with his lips pressed together that

suggested I was behaving like a tiresome child.

"Your line of thinking is absolutely correct, but I'm still going to joke about it," I chuckled.

"Fair enough," he shrugged. "The boys don't much care between pirating or straight work, as long as they have food and a home, but you know they prefer keeping safe." He looked at me with a kind smile. "Twas good of you to take the young lads on board."

I shrugged, watching Teeth and Davy on their knees in the sand. They were crawling around, obeying Flora's every command as they gathered what she needed.

"I don't know how a man's to get any experience if nobody gives him a first chance," I said. "They're good boys. Certainly rough around the edges, but over the past few years they've proven themselves."

"That they have," O'Doule agreed. "And if you'll forgive me saying it, Captain, I'd rather not have them risking jail or worse with the thieving anymore."

"Aye. That's the main reason I knew it was time to shift gears," I nodded. "Not to mention that you and McGee are getting up in years," I winked.

"Foul bugger," he muttered under his breath. But the spark in his eye told me that my friend and crewmate would always forgive my sass.

***

~ Chapter 13 ~ Flora ~

* On the way to Tegarren Point *

It was fascinating that I was nearly always aware of the time of day, but couldn't really keep track of how many days had passed. The angle of the sun told me whether I should hurry up and finish the section of sewing I was working on so that I could go help with supper. The tiny bit of daylight creeping through the Captain's bedroom window told me that it was time to jump up, dress, and head down to the galley to start breakfast.

I was incredibly proud that I had made myself a new dress that I could pull on and off myself, with no constricting buttons down the back. It was not fashionable, in a silvery gray like the soft light of dawn. It was not particularly flattering. It was simply a dress for working comfortably and living on this ship.

Never in my life would I have believed that I would jump up in the morning, eager to be the first person working. There was something so calming about the ritual of scrubbing the table, stoking the fire, putting the kettle on, and starting the morning before the men awoke.

Back at home, nothing I ever did was good enough. The food I cooked was too bland, dinner was too slow, and somehow I never laid anything out on the plate properly. My sewing work was not fast enough, and my father would point out errors that did not exist.

Here on the Fortune, the men complimented me on my cooking every single day. Even when Teeth didn't like it, he appreciated trying something new.

Larry had handed all of the sail work and sewing over to me. I created patterns for shirts for the men, using an old one for a template, and my memory of my mother's projects. Luckily, Davy and Teeth were approximately the same size, though Teeth was shorter, as were O'Doule and McGee. Larry and the Captain were a similar width, though Larry was even taller. So I was able to make do with three main patterns, saving a lot of time. I would probably be able to present them all with their new shirts in about a week.

McGee said that he would be starting supper this evening, since he was finished with his barrel repairs early. That gave me extra time to finish the cuff of a shirt sleeve.

It was so peaceful working away steadily, occasionally looking out the tiny window to see the rolling sea and the expansive sky. The world seemed so much bigger out here. It was a beautiful feeling.

A quick, sharp yell cut through the peaceful lapping of the waves against the hull.

Nearly dropping my buttons, I raced along with the other men to find McGee holding his hand, which was covered in blood.

Instantly O'Doule went to work, sitting him down and grabbing clean rags to wrap his finger tightly, raising it up over his head and squeezing tight.

"Clear out, boys, I've got this," O'Doule ordered. Everyone left immediately, a few of them looking a bit pale.

But I stayed. "My mother taught me some things," I said quickly. "I could help if you like."

"Aye, grab me a mug, and pour in two splashes from the clear bottle on the bottom shelf."

As I pulled the cork and poured, I caught a whiff of something that was even sharper than the rum. Handing it to O'Doule, he lowered McGee's hand, wiping off the blood then splashing some of the liquid along the cut.

It hurt my heart to see McGee's teeth grinding together as he stifled a yell. Whatever it was, it must have stung something fierce. O'Doule handed him the mug and he drank down the rest.

"Bloody northerners and their potato swill," McGee growled.

"Prevents infection," O'Doule said sternly. I brought the lamp over so that he could examine the wound more closely. "Bugger it. Lad, you really sliced yourself deep."

McGee hung his head. "The blasted knife slipped and somehow I caught it with both hands."

O'Doule cocked his head, thinking. "We might have to wrap this tight, and get you to the doc in Tegarren Point for some stitches."

I leaned closer, examining the straight line of the cut. "I can do it," I offered. They both looked at me in shock.

"I had to stitch a cut on my mother's back once, from where… It doesn't matter. It's the same as sewing, you simply run the needle through the flame of the lamp first to make sure it's clean."

McGee nodded. "Better now than tomorrow, and better you than a stranger, I suppose."

I ran to fetch a needle and thread, then came back to run the needle through the flame. O'Doule poured McGee a measure of rum, and he drank it in one swig.

I wiped down his hand as well as I could, stretching it out across the table with cloths underneath. "The good news is, this should only take a few minutes," I said. "The bad news is, it might sting like the devil, and it might give you the willies something fierce."

"Do you need me to stay to hold his hand down, lass?" O'Doule asked.

I looked McGee in the eye. "Will you keep still?" He nodded very seriously.

"Good," said O'Doule. "Then I'll tell the Captain we don't need to rush as much to Tegarren Point. I can hear him planning to hoist the extra sails, yet it's a bad time of the evening for it."

He left quickly, and I saw McGee tense his arm, while

looking away. "Go ahead, Miss. I might mutter some rather blue words, but I won't move."

I could barely stomach the next part, but I had to. Like when I was stitching up my mother, I had to put aside my squeamish feelings, and simply attend to the task at hand. Taking a deep breath in, and blowing it out slowly, I gripped McGee's skin, and began to sew.

It was obvious that McGee's teeth were grinding together, and he could barely stand the sting. "Look up to the ceiling, never at what I'm doing," I said quickly. "What is your mother's name?"

His head twitched and he seemed confused, but I just kept stitching steadily, as quickly as I could. "Patricia," he said, his voice slightly raspy.

"Tell me all about the best meal that she ever made for the holidays when you were young."

He didn't question my diversion tactic, launching into extravagant detail about her turkey dinner with stuffing, pumpkin pie, and molasses glazed rosemary carrots. By the time he was finished, so was I. Tearing the cleanest rag into strips, I wrapped his finger and hand as snuggly as I could.

"If the pressure is too tight in an hour, let me know and I'll loosen it off a bit," I said.

He nodded, his breathing more steady now that the painful part was over. I began scrubbing everything up while he took a moment to collect himself.

"Now, my mother said that garlic and onion are good for fighting infections," I said, "So I'll cook with those for the next few days, and give you extra. I'll be making dinner tonight, as you can't get that wet or dirty."

"Yes, thank you, Miss," McGee said. I couldn't be sure if the usually outspoken man was being meek due to the pain of the stitches, or that he wasn't used to being so near a woman for so long.

He extended his other hand, and I returned the gesture automatically. He brought his lips to the back of my hand in a tiny kiss. "Thank you, m'lady. I greatly appreciate this."

Just then the Captain came around the corner, and McGee dropped my hand, looking ashen. "Cap'n, your fine lass can sew more than clothing." He held up his bandaged hand.

The Captain's lips were tight, and he didn't speak.

"A dozen wee stitches, right through me skin, Cap'n. Just like a real doctor."

"Good job, lass," the Captain said curtly. "Back to work with ye, McGee."

"Yessir." He disappeared up onto the deck.

I tidied up the supplies and scrubbed the table clean, while the Captain just stared at me. Finally I turned to look at him. "Is there a problem, sir?"

He pulled out a barrel and sat, pulling me onto his lap. "No problem with you, lassie. It was... unsettling to see another man kiss you."

I laughed lightly. "Sir, I had just been piercing his skin with a needle. He was not in his right mind, and I think the tender gesture was purely gratitude."

"Aye. Still didn't like it." He appeared uncomfortable, still tense.

My eyes darted around, making sure we were alone. Wrapping my hands around his neck, I brought our mouths close as I whispered, "You're the only man I've really kissed." Our lips met, and his arms pulled me in until I was pressed tightly against him.

I couldn't believe how I felt his kisses through my entire body. It felt like he was possessing me through his lips. Overtaking me gently. Completely.

In my close-fitting, light dress, he could see my arousal immediately, as the peaks of my nipples stood out clearly. His palm slid along my back, then under my arm to circle my breast. My tiny gasp against his lips was pure excitement, and I could feel his kiss turn into a smile. His large hand cupped the weight of my soft skin as I melted against him. Bringing his thumb across the peak of my nipple, he made me sigh too loudly.

Realizing that we could be caught at any moment, he

retracted his hand and leaned back. He seemed amused by the way I pouted.

"Not the time nor the place, lassie," he said, bouncing me on his knee jovially. "Not appropriate to let the lads see what they cannot have."

Pressing my lips together in thought, I contemplated for a moment.

"Ask your question, lass."

"Sir, I know that men have needs. Does, um... does the ship pull into certain ports occasionally so that the men can go..." I lowered my voice to below a breath, "Whoring?"

His laugh was so loud and bright that it startled me. "Aye, lassie, 'tis true. The minds of men become those of squirrels if they don't feel the touch of a woman every so often. Does this bother you?"

I shook my head. "Not at all. I was just curious." I didn't tell him that fragments of stories had accidentally reached my ears since I'd been onboard. I also didn't tell him how intriguing I thought the stories were.

He suddenly looked a bit forlorn. "A proper lass like you really shouldn't know about such things, nor hear the language of six salty sailors all day."

"Nonsense," I said, standing up and putting away the rags to be scrubbed later. "I've learned more in my weeks on this ship than I have in the past five years in the village." I winked. "And I don't just mean the bawdy talk."

After supper, I felt like the men couldn't talk freely with me there, so I took a lamp to the Captain's bedroom and worked on my little shell collars. I knew that the men probably needed some lads only time.

I couldn't help that a few of the more boisterous bits of the conversation reached my ears. They were indeed planning to visit a port sometime soon that featured their favorite whorehouse. I'd heard a few whispers on deck, but once they were into the rum, things became louder.

Although I tried to concentrate on my work, that had me in a bit of a tizzy. I felt so close to the Captain, but it was hard to tell how he felt about me.

In the beginning, I'd assume that since he had purchased me, he'd use me to satisfy his carnal desires. Then I realized how gentle and kind he was to me. He had to know that now that I knew him, that's what I wanted as well. Or was I so shy and reserved that I hadn't been clear with my feelings toward him?

It was times like these when I wished that I had a girlfriend to talk to about such matters.

***

~ Chapter 14 ~ The Captain ~

* *The Rum* *

It didn't take much persuasion before I was drinking an extra bit of rum and telling some of the tales I likely should have kept to myself.

Like the time we outran the Navy's fastest new ship on its maiden voyage. Then we informed everyone at their first port of call before they reached it so they'd be a laughing stock. It was simply a tale too amusing not to tell for the hundredth time.

When the laughter died down, McGee piped up. "Do you think I'll get an injured sailor discount in a few weeks down at Walton's Hotel?" he inquired, holding up his bandaged hand.

We all burst into uproarious laughter again. Walton's was a very discreet hotel, where only those in the know would walk up to the third floor to the house of ill repute. A lounge full of lovely ladies of the evening waited there to entertain sailors for a fair price.

The conversation grew loud and rowdy, with some of the men describing their favorite ladies in naughty detail. A great debate broke out, and sides were taken over which was more glorious, Kitty's bosom or Emily's arse.

"'Tis a ripe peach," Teeth grinned, his gold smile shining in the lamplight. "When you give it a little spank and a squeeze, it's heaven on earth."

"'Tis fine indeed," McGee agreed, "But Kitty's bosom defies gravity itself. Melons so delicious you'd best take a bite."

The boys had been so well behaved around Miss Flora that I had to allow their tongues to get loose once in a while, and joined them in laughing like fools.

I noticed Larry giving me a bit of an odd look from the corner of his eye. "Ask your question, mate."

"I know that you don't always join us down at Walton's," he said carefully. "I just wondered whether you'd be coming along this time or not?"

Clapping him on the back, I shook my head. "No, I shan't, and I'm sure you know why."

I noticed some covert glances around the table. "Speak up, boys. We have no secrets here."

Davy cleared his throat. "Well, sir, we sort of assumed that with you purchasing Miss Flora, she might become your… er, mistress. But we've seen no evidence of, shall we say, togetherness between you that wasn't fairly innocent."

Staring into my mug, I swirled my rum around, not sure of how to answer honestly. "You all know at first I just wanted to save her." The crew all nodded.

"Aye, Captain, and you were right to do so," O'Doule agreed.

"But then I got to know the wee lass." I paused. It felt like everyone had grown beyond silent.

Then I shook my head. "If we had a normal life, and I were a respectable villager, I would court her, as she is a proper lady. But having her suddenly thrown into my life, and my bed, things are a bit strange."

The lads all nodded. "Yes, odd circumstances indeed," Larry said.

"I would never want to scare the sweet lass, or make her feel obligated in any way. So for now, I'm simply going to take my time…" I winked. "And be sure that she falls madly in love with me."

I drained my mug while the lads cheered and laughed.

"Good plan," Teeth agreed. "I'd like her to stay around. And I don't just say that because I do like most of her cooking."

I saw that McGee almost swatted him in the arm, then thought better of it when he remembered his fresh stitches.

"She really has worked out to be a good member of the crew," O'Doule said. "She jumped right in to be our doctor when we needed her. That was a bit of a surprise."

I nodded. "Yes, she is full of surprises, I do agree."

Pushing away from the table, I stood up. "And on that note, I should go make sure that she has stopped working for the night. The precious little thing is going to cause her sewing fingers to fall right off."

A chorus of, "G'night, Captain," filled the room as I waved behind me, heading to my quarters.

Sure enough, my sweet little Flora was there, working on her necklaces. "Sweetheart, I worry that you work yourself too hard."

She looked up at me with a smile, then her bright eyes grew wide. I realized I might not have called her that before.

Sitting beside her, I tipped her chin up to mine with a finger. "You are my little sweetheart, aren't you?"

Those big blue eyes regarded me carefully, then she nodded. Her soft lips turned up in a tiny smile, then I kissed her.

Every time we kissed it felt like we were dissolving into each other even more. As if we needed to crawl into each other's skin and become one person. It was astounding how much this little lass meant to me in such a short time.

***

~ Chapter 15 ~ Flora ~

In the Dark

I heard a few fragments of conversation about the hotel some of the lads would be visiting soon. This made my stomach feel like it was being tied in knots.

I had no problem with the thought of a brothel. I knew that men had needs. If they didn't have a wife, they would naturally look into other ways of fulfilling those needs. If a lady chose to be paid for her intimate company, that was her own business, not mine.

Yet the thought of the Captain with another woman filled me with a fit of strange, sickening anger that I'd never experienced before. I had been slightly jealous of school friends who were allowed more freedom than I was, and of those who were able to eat as much as they wanted. But this didn't feel like jealousy. It felt like terror and rage stirring together in my belly, the mixture becoming poison.

If the Captain wanted to visit ladies who knew what they were doing in the bedroom, it wasn't my place to stop him. But perhaps I could please him enough that he'd not want to bother with them? Why pay for ladies of the evening, when he had already paid so much for me?

Somehow it was easier to think of doing my duty and pleasing him rather than admitting the truth to myself. I wanted him because I wanted him. Completely. He told me that the sea was a place where people could take what they wanted, with no regrets. I needed his touch in a way that was brand new for me. I didn't understand it. Maybe I didn't have to.

Unless of course he didn't want me in that way, and I was just an amusement that kept him entertained until he visited the hotel again. For all I knew, he could have a regular lady there. Or wish to visit a new one every time.

I hated not knowing a darn thing about the workings of men's minds. In a way, it wasn't my place. But I hated feeling like I was in the dark.

Yet as he called me his sweetheart and kissed me, I felt my worries fade away a bit. Instead of relaxing, however, the heat in our kiss grew and grew. The Captain swept me off my feet, laying me across the bed.

Without even thinking, I quickly unbuttoned his shirt, spreading my fingers as I moved my hands across his muscled chest.

Something came over me. I don't think it was the fear of losing him to another woman. I think it was the intoxicating desire of wanting him for myself. Then I realized he wasn't stopping me.

He helped me pull his shirt off, then sat me up and helped me remove my dress. Laying under him in nothing but my knickers, my heart was beating far too fast. His kisses became softer, his lips gliding against mine as my hand reached up to grip the back of his hair. It thrilled me to hear a low growl escape his throat.

"Lassie, whatever am I going to do with you?" He smiled seductively, his deep eyes meeting mine as he seemed to ponder for a moment.

"I'm yours," I whispered. "Do whatever you like with me, sir."

His eyes closed for a moment, and I felt a shudder run through him. "There is a little something I've been craving, my sweet girl."

"Anything," I breathed. From the way he was looking at me, I knew that anything he wanted to do would be incredible.

His lips crushed to mine, kissing me so hard it nearly took my breath away. His large hands caressed my breasts gently, as he swirled his thumbs over my tender nipples.

My tiny cries against his mouth seemed to amuse him. Then he began kissing along my jaw, and down my neck. I gripped the back of his shoulders as his tongue swirled around my breast. It was hard not to shriek when his teeth gently tugged at my nipple, teasing me with a little pinch. I barely noticed when he tugged off my knickers until I instinctively spread my thighs a bit.

"You're the most beautiful woman I've ever seen, Flora," he whispered, moving to the other side to skim his tongue along my delicate peak until I moaned. "Quiet, you hot little thing," he smiled up at me. "The boys are still awake."

I wasn't sure why having to be silent made what he was doing even more exciting. It was our naughty secret. His firm kisses wandered down my stomach, stopping at the top of my mound as he looked up at me with a wink. I was stunned as he spread me wide open with his broad shoulders, settling between my legs.

His thick fingers danced along my most delicate skin, gently caressing me while I tried to breathe. I was flooded with feelings I couldn't make sense of. It felt like my insides were becoming juicy and soft. My entire body was melting, and I gasped as his slippery tongue licked firmly through my crease.

"You're positively delicious, my darling lass," he murmured.

He curled his tongue around my oversensitive nub of skin in a way that drove me half crazy. Then I felt his finger dipping into my moisture, beginning to stroke inside me very carefully. The bliss was building through my center, and it felt like lightning was flashing through my veins.

When he managed to wiggle his finger all the way inside, he began to stroke gently all the way in and out. I couldn't believe the sensation of fullness, and once again felt like I was dangling from the edge of a cliff, about to fall into the sea.

Flattening his tongue against my sensitive bit of nerves, the Captain looked up at me with fire in his eyes.

I couldn't speak. I couldn't catch my breath. As he added a second finger, thrusting slowly in and out of my snug passage,

I felt heat blaze through me. Then I was falling, twitching, complete bliss washing through me as I quivered, squealing beneath him. His other hand clapped over my mouth as I wailed, my fingers clutching his hair as I pulled his mouth firmly against me.

As the wave of complete release overtook me, I felt drained and energized at the same time. When I finally stopped twitching, the Captain looked up at me and licked his lips. "My lovely girl, you're as sweet as I expected."

Pulling him by the hair, he chuckled at my urgency as I pulled his lips to mine. I needed to feel him on top of me. My legs wrapped around his hips as I yanked him against me, rocking against his body with pure, raw need.

"You adorable little temptress," he smiled.

He rolled onto his side so that he didn't crush me, even though I was enjoying the feeling immensely. He shoved off his pants, snuggling against me completely naked.

My hand instantly reached for his arousal, and I loved the feeling of his tough, hard body against mine as he clutched me close. Stroking his length, I felt him grow under my touch as he became even more firm.

Rolling slightly, the Captain laid on his back, possibly hoping that I would use both hands again. But after the unbelievable feeling of his mouth on my intimate parts, I could only imagine that he would appreciate the same.

Kissing him gently, I swiped the palm of my hand against the tip of his shaft lightly, teasing him until I could feel the smile in his lips.

Then I kissed down his chest quickly, holding his rigid pole in both hands as I wrapped my rosy lips around the top. He looked down at me with an expression of complete astonishment.

Sticking out my tongue saucily, I circled around the bulbous head, caressing him gently as I massaged the rest with my hands. I saw his rippled stomach tighten as his body curled forward slightly.

Feeling such a big man under my control like this was so

unusual. I couldn't possibly deny how much I liked it.

Opening my mouth as wide as I could, I felt my lips stretch around his skin as I rubbed the tip of his shaft against my tongue. His eyes blazed, and I felt his hand gently stroke the back of my hair.

I wanted to make him as happy as he'd made me over the past several weeks. Feeling his shaft begin to twitch, I opened wider, thrusting his length into my mouth, then bobbing up and down. Pressing my lips against his skin, I tried to touch him more firmly. It looked like he was nearly gasping for air, as his hand grasped the back of my head.

Moving even faster, I created a slight sucking motion, pressing as much of his flesh down my throat as I could.

Looking up to meet his eyes, they were only half open, unfocused as he choked, "Flora…" Then his stomach seemed to clench as his organ spasmed, shooting his seed straight down my throat as I swallowed quickly.

I licked him clean, feeling that it was the polite thing to do. Then I slowly pulled my hands away, looking up at him hopefully.

The Captain's eyes were glazed as he seemed to be pleased beyond measure. "My lovely lass, wherever did you learn a trick like that?"

I felt myself blushing hotly. "I've never done that before, sir. I just thought you might like it."

He pulled me up beside him, wrapping an arm around my shoulders. "It's been ages since I've felt anything half as nice, I assure you."

He leaned over to kiss me, and I felt so tiny under his huge frame. Pulling him on top of me, the feeling of his weight upon me stirred my insides, filling every part of my body with the deepest longing. His tongue entwined with mine, as I spread my legs, rocking against him with pure, raw need.

"You're insatiable," he purred, his lips against the hollow of my throat.

"I've never felt like this before," I breathed.

"That's because you're free here, lass. You can just let go."

I needed to feel his length between my legs. It was a strange urge that radiated outward from my insides, demanding that I obey.

Just when I thought I felt a flutter from his manhood, he shifted me so that I was lying beside him again. His hand squeezed my breast firmly, sending shivers through me. Then his hand lowered, and I eagerly spread my thighs for his fingers.

"You have no idea what it does to me, knowing that you need my touch, lass."

I couldn't form words, simply moaning softly as he entered me with two fingers, stretching me open. Without thinking, I laid my leg over his hips, opening wider.

"That's it," he murmured, kissing along my ear, my cheekbone. "Open for me, sweetheart."

His fingers began thrusting harder, faster, and if I hadn't been lying down my knees would have buckled. Then his thumb pressed against my secret little spot, and my entire body began to rock against him.

"Yes," a harsh, breathy cry escaped me. "Please… yes…"

He kissed me softly, wetly, our mouths holding us together even though my body began to nearly thrash. I held his shoulders, my fingernails digging into his skin as the dam within me broke open, spilling warm golden pleasure through every part of me.

"Oh… Captain," I choked. Tremors ran through me until I eventually became still, seeing stars behind my eyelids.

"My precious girl. You are so beautiful, but when you're in the midst of joy, you're just radiant."

My heart felt like it had melted into a puddle, swishing around inside my chest. These feelings were growing each day, but every time our bodies were close, the bonds grew intensely. The way he was looking at me so sweetly, rocking me in his arms, I felt completely at peace.

Suddenly he laughed heartily, shaking me and surprising me at once. "My word, lassie, you poor little thing. Are you afraid I'd be going out with the lads to the bawdy house the week after next?"

I bit my lip nervously. "It's not my place to ask, sir."

"My dear girl," he said gently, taking my hand in his and placing it against his heart. "How could I look at another woman when I have the prettiest lass in the land right here beside me?"

Feeling tears prick the corners of my eyes, I shut them tightly for a moment. When I opened them, he was still smiling warmly. He kissed my nose, making me giggle.

"You're my girl, Flora. I'll never want for another."

I felt my face flushing, even under my faint new sun-kissed glow.

"Flora, look at me."

I stared into his deep, nearly black eyes. His desire, his longing, was all right there. It was like seeing into his mind.

"Little lass, the day your bastard father marched you to my ship was the best day of my life." Then he chuckled. "Ol' Cap'n Yarlie used to say that some of the best things in life were the ones you stumbled into ass-backward."

He lifted my hand and touched it to his lips. "We were meant to be, little one. I'm greatly relieved that you've taken to a life at sea like a duck to water."

I nodded eagerly. "You've been so kind to me, sir. And all of the men have been very understanding and helpful. I can honestly say, although it's only my second, this is the best home I've ever had."

He nodded, snuggling me into his chest as he wrapped the blankets around us. "You're my home now, Flora," he whispered against my hair.

***

~ Chapter 16 ~ The Captain ~

Quick Stop in Parrinport

It was already our fourth trip back to Parrinport so that Flora could sell her necklaces and other jewelry things.

The shopkeeper from the fabric store had apparently coordinated with the local dress shop. Now they were both selling sea-themed accessories to all of the ladies in several of the neighboring towns. They were creating their own little fashion district, of a sort.

I would never pretend to know a thing about styles, but it certainly seemed that Flora's inventions were very distinct. It wasn't just her use of shells and beach stones. It was the way she added just a touch of blue or a drop of green in the form of a ribbon or button.

From what little I'd noticed, the other women, especially the older ones, seemed to make brash statements, like a bright yellow hat. Flora was more thoughtful, creating a wee clip a lady might wear in her hair. Or a pin for the front of her dress to make it look fancier without having to change the whole dress.

It was all a bit confusing to me, but what was clear was that Flora was flourishing. She insisted on still doing the ship's work for most of the day, then she worked afternoons and evenings on her ladies' things.

Somehow, she didn't look tired at all. She looked radiantly happy. I hadn't caught her without a smile on her face for weeks. Every time she came back to the docks after dropping off her packages at the shop, she was absolutely beaming.

It was sweet that she kept wanting to give me the money she earned, but I'd have none of that. It seemed like this was probably the first time she had a few coins of her own, and she should keep them for herself.

This trip, watching her practically skip back up the dock toward me, I couldn't resist pulling her up into my arms for a giant hug. Larry was trailing her, as always, and politely looked away for a moment so I could give Flora a tiny kiss.

Setting her down, I asked, "How did it go today, lass?"

"Wonderful, sir. Both of the women bought absolutely everything and asked for much more. They were very grateful I could get everything to them this weekend, since they have a festival next week."

"But you told them it might be a spell before we return?" I asked.

"Of course. I wouldn't want you to make extra trips on my account."

I might not have mentioned that this particular trip had mostly been for her. Certainly, we had a few other deliveries and shipments to attend to, but her business was the focus this time around.

"I'm much more concerned about you working too hard," I said, wrapping an arm around her as I walked her onto the ship. "I don't want our sweet girl to go blind from your tiny work in the lamplight, or wearing those pretty fingers to the bone."

She grinned up at me. "It's sweet that you're concerned, but I promise that I'm fine." She took her packages from Larry and scampered off to stow them away.

Turning to Larry, I asked, "It sounds like those shopkeepers really adore her trinkets?"

"Aye, they do," he said, his huge grin creasing his scar up higher. "This time the fabric store lady had what seemed to be her husband in the shop as well. I think he wanted to meet Flora. I was over by the front door, so I didn't hear much of their conversation, but they all seemed delighted with her."

Clapping him on the shoulder, I said, "I truly appreciate

you looking out for her."

"Of course, sir." He looked slightly uncomfortable for a second before he added, "We can't very well have your face walking around this town in case those posters are still up."

"It was a long time ago. Beyond that, it makes me feel secure that you are the one looking out for her. I know you would do anything to keep her safe."

The huge man nodded as he looked slightly down at me, flashing his endearing grin. "Miss Flora has become like a sister to me," he said softly. "I'm not ashamed to say she has brought a bit of home comfort to the ship, sir."

"I agree. But she does work those wee hands too hard, so how about you and I go scrub the potatoes?"

When Flora joined us to cook supper, she laughed merrily as Larry and I pretended she was the Captain of Dinner. We obeyed her every command, which also amused the boys as they gathered around the table.

It was a wonderful supper, with everyone telling their own little tales of what happened in the village today. Teeth and McGee had been delivering packages of spices to a restaurant, and were given buttery sugar cookies by the chef. While Davey and O'Doule were delivering a shipment of grain to a nearby stable, they saw the tallest white horse they'd ever seen.

"'Twas like a mythical creature," Davy exclaimed, wide-eyed. "If it had suddenly taken off and flown away, I would not have been surprised."

O'Doule grinned. "Normally I'd say the lad was pulling your leg, Captain, but this was a magnificent beast indeed. It must have been at least seventeen hands tall. I would have paid good money to see it run full speed."

I was just about to inquire what such a sight would be worth to him, when we heard hollering up on deck.

"What sort of savage interrupts the supper hour?" I grumbled. I nodded to Larry, and he followed me up to see seven uniformed policemen about to board my ship.

"Hold up, gentlemen," I said with a wide smile. I raised

my hands slightly, allowing my coat to flare out so they could see I was unarmed. When a man is outnumbered, it's best to begin by being social and putting them at ease.

"How may I help you officers this evening?" I asked, in a calm tone that suggested I expected their request to be reasonable.

"Are you the Captain of The Toothy Scallywag?"

I scrunched up my face to appear as confused as possible, then gestured to the side of the ship. "'Tis The Fortune's Favor, as you can see right here on the hull."

The officers looked between each other, less certain. "We have a warrant for the arrest of the Captain of The Toothy Scallywag, and believe you match the picture on the wanted posters."

"Well, you can plainly see I am the Captain of a different ship." I gestured to my face. "Perhaps this mug is simply preferred by your poster artist."

I flashed them a broad grin, making three of the officers in the back almost choke from trying to stifle their chuckles.

"The Mayor of Parrinport can confirm your identity," the head officer said.

"Fine. Where is he? And does he prefer rum or ale?" I asked brightly.

The head cop scowled. "He happens to be out of town on business, but he'll be back tomorrow afternoon."

"Well, that's lovely. My navigator says the weather will be mighty fine tomorrow. We could have a picnic together."

This time one of the officers in the back chuckled out loud, causing their leader to glare daggers at him.

"I didn't realize I was an important enough fellow to garner a meeting with your Mayor," I said. "But I will certainly clear my schedule for it."

The head officer gave me a flat look. "We won't be trusting you not to sail off. We'll throw you in the jail until the Mayor arrives."

I cocked my head, considering. "Now, I mean absolutely no disrespect, but I'm just guessing that our cook is better than your cook. So if you wouldn't mind me finishing my supper first…"

The head police officer snapped his fingers, and five of them grabbed me. But since four of them were snickering, I had a feeling they were not as rough as they could have been with a man suspected of piracy.

Larry lunged for me, but I quickly shook my head. I knew that he could throw the lot of them overboard in seconds, but I didn't want to think of the younger ones getting hurt. I also didn't want to think of what would happen if they called in reinforcements, or pulled out pistols. Or began examining the Fortune from stem to stern. Especially since some of the paint from the new name of the ship was beginning to flake off in patches.

I stood up as straight as possible, then walked very slowly down the plank, nodding at Larry with a huge smile. "You'll have to finish my supper for me, mate. Tell the tiny one not to worry. This will all be sorted tomorrow."

As I marched smartly down the dock, I inquired of the officer holding my left arm, "Honestly now, does the Mayor prefer rum or ale? When I invite him back to the ship for a drink after this all blows over, I'll need to know what to serve him."

***

~ Chapter 17 ~ Flora ~

After Supper

I heard men's voices up on deck, but it sounded like the Captain was jovial. Still, my curiosity got the better of me.

The other men didn't say a word as I crept up the stairs, peeking out to see a handful of uniformed men grabbing the Captain. He was behaving as if it was all some sort of joke or ruse.

Larry looked angry enough to smack all of their heads together, but the Captain seemed to stop him with one glance. Before I knew what was happening, the Captain was being marched away. Larry turned to come back downstairs and saw my horrified face.

"What happened?" I could barely whisper.

Larry tried to smile, then sagged, shaking his head. "Sometimes a man's past life catches up with him," he said sadly, leading me back down to the others.

We sat down, and from the looks shot around the table, it seemed like only Larry, O'Doule, and McGee had a clue what was going on.

"We know that in his younger days the Captain was a bit of a squirrelly pirate," Larry said slowly. "Before he decided to become a respectable trader and shipper, this vessel sailed under another name, and a much different set of rules."

O'Doule nodded. "I would have thought that the Mayor of this town would have been long gone by now. But yes, there was an incident here. The Captain didn't show his face around these parts for several years."

"We were sure it would have been safe by now," McGee said thoughtfully. "Memories fade. Wanted posters fade. Unless maybe that was the only interesting incident that has ever occurred around here?"

O'Doule shrugged. "No matter. We'll have to figure something out."

"The Mayor won't be back until tomorrow afternoon," Larry said. "So at least we have tonight."

Everyone settled in to think hard, but my mind was spinning and bouncing like an apple rolling down a hill. I knew it was probably my fault we were here. I had wondered if the Captain had been making extra trips on my account. By coming here on a regular basis, it must have alerted the authorities.

Perhaps the Mayor himself had come down for a stroll while the Captain was on deck. Or perhaps rumors had spread that the ship had been renamed. I didn't know how these things worked, but there couldn't be many ships of this size that made runs around the area.

"Oh my goodness," I whispered.

"What is it, Miss?" Larry asked softly.

"The man who was in the fabric store."

"The shopkeeper's husband?"

I shook my head. "I assumed that's who he was, but it could've been the Mayor himself, or someone in his family. Remember his very expensive looking suit?"

Larry shrugged. "If his wife runs the shop, he should have the best clothing, I would think."

"When he wanted to shake my hand to thank me for the brisk sales they were doing, he asked my name." I looked up to Larry, blinking hard as my eyes swam with tears. "And he asked the name of the ship I was from."

O'Doule reached across the table to pat my hand. "Lass, any of the dock men could have mentioned what ships were in port."

"But the shopkeeper could have told him we were there often. They could have been expecting us. Is this all my fault?"

I collapsed into my folded arms on the table, sobbing uncontrollably. Although I felt both Larry and Davy's hands stroking my back, it was little comfort.

If it was my fault that the wonderful man who had transformed my entire life was in jail, I didn't know if I could ever forgive myself.

***

~ Chapter 18 ~ The Captain ~

* *Limestone Walls* *

Sometimes a tiny bit of information can be dangerous, without the rest of the information available to fill out the picture.

The authorities probably knew that a ship would never leave without its Captain on board. But they were probably too ignorant to realize that my men wouldn't just stay on the ship waiting around.

An hour after I had been unceremoniously dumped into a jail cell, a pebble came flying through the open window above. It was far higher than I could ever reach, but it was certainly enough to send a signal.

If I threw the pebble back, it confirmed that I was indeed here, but unable to speak freely. Yet with no other prisoners and the guard down the hall, it was all clear.

"Davy," I said sharply, looking up at the dim square of gray above.

"Captain. Are you alright?"

"Aye, clean and dry."

I heard him snort, containing his chuckles. "Strength?"

I had already checked the cell. The floor and walls were made of limestone, the bars of solid steel. "Fortress," I said, indicating that there was no way I could break out with physical force.

"Numbers?"

"One," I said, telling him that there was only one guard left on duty.

"Others?"

"Nay."

"Hold tight," Davy called.

"Aye."

Other men might be panicking in this situation. I was simply curious. Everything would pan out one way or the other. Perhaps my crew would find a way to break down the front door, overpower the guard, and bust me out.

Or perhaps they would weigh all of the information, and decide it would be better to wait until the Mayor was arriving, and cause some sort of grand diversion so that I could run off. They might even sail a short distance east, leaving one man here to coordinate with me, then we would steal a tiny boat to catch up to them.

No matter what happened, I knew they'd find a way.

I hated to admit that this was one part of pirating I missed, just a tiny bit. I didn't like using weapons, or transporting a lot of explosives. I really didn't like stealing at all, but especially not from regular folk.

There were aspects of the pirates' life that were perfectly suited to me, but many that weren't. Yet there was something about the little bits of adventure that fired up my blood.

My only deep regret was knowing that Flora must be worried sick. When I got out of this predicament, I would vow to put even more distance between the old life and the new.

It wasn't right of me to put her through such worry. How could I have her falling in love with me if she couldn't trust me? How could she give me her heart if I couldn't guarantee I would always be there for her?

I would never have dreamed that I would love a woman more than my ship, more than my own life. Now I pictured Flora in my arms, her sweet gentle face tipped up to mine as she opened herself completely. My little angel deserved much better.

Sitting in the dark on the floor of a stone jail cell, I grinned to myself.

I was completely in love with Flora. I was no longer a pirate. And I was deeply joyous about both of those revelations.

Haley Travis

***

~ Chapter 19 ~ Flora ~

* A Plan *

The hour was growing late as Davy came back and joined us. Sitting around the table, the crew all stared at the wooden surface, and each other. My hands were still visibly shaking.

In all my life, I'd never dared to think I'd fall in love. My future had seemed so certain. My father would marry me off, and I'd have to plaster a smile on my face, and do as I was told.

It was a bizarre twist of the fates that I should be sold to a man who made me feel so much so fast. A man who lifted me up. Made me feel precious and adored. A man who wanted me to explore the world however I liked, and share things together.

There was no way I was going to let him waste even one night in jail, away from me.

Davy kindly held out his mug of rum. "Here, Miss. Take one sip. It'll calm your nerves."

"Thank you," I whispered, taking my first swallow of rum ever. Handing the mug back, I tried not to sputter, choking it down. "How can liquid burn so much?" I squeaked.

At least I made the men laugh, which brightened the mood.

"Alright, men," Larry said. "And Miss."

I grinned, blinking hard as my eyes started to water again, this time from the roaring flush of heat tingling through me instead of tears.

"We've never lost a man, and we're certainly not going

to lose our Captain." Everyone nodded, looking determined. "This is an older town," Larry explained, "So the jail is likely fortified, and we can't expect the Captain to break out."

"Aye," Davy said. "He said it's solid, but only one guard."

Larry nodded. "We'll need to break him out then. And it must be tonight, before they gather the authorities in the morning. If the townspeople find out that they're holding a… smuggler, shall we say, they'll all come down for the spectacle."

"Aye, then there will be eyes everywhere," O'Doule said, nodding. "So, it's tonight. Let's think of our options."

"Do we have any explosives left?" Teeth asked.

"No, we used those up blowing the lock on the treasure chests back in Claytonsfield," McGee said. "Captain doesn't want us to carry much of that anymore."

O'Doule shook his head. "Let's start with non-violent options. Can anyone pick locks?"

"House locks, yes," Davy said. "The normal sort of little lock on a home or a stable, I can open. But the jail would have a bolt lock at the front door, and a sturdy lock on the cell where they're holding him." He shook his head sadly, the edge of his headscarf flapping slightly. "I could try, but it might take me a very long time."

Larry shrugged. "I could easily break in the front door, since that's likely wood. But I can't throw myself at steel bars."

"Well, ye could," chuckled Teeth. "But you'd have bruises like tiger stripes for days."

"I've heard of guards in many towns being bribed," O'Doule said, tapping his fingers on the table. "But it would take a great amount. Only the Captain would have that much coin, and he'd have it well hidden."

"How much?" I asked, trying hard to make my voice sound steady.

"Perhaps fifteen to twenty gold coins or so," he said.

"I'll be right back," I said, dashing to the Captain's quarters.

I'd been keeping the profits from the necklace and jewelry sales in a little cloth bag, hidden under my old dress on a shelf. I had tried to give it to the Captain, but he refused. So I just let it build up. I hadn't bothered counting it for some time.

Dashing back to the galley, I emptied the bag onto the table. O'Doule shot me a look, then began counting. I found it amusing that he didn't ask where the money came from. The rest of the men simply stared at the money.

"This is from the jewelry sales," I said quickly. "I haven't spent a cent."

Larry immediately patted my shoulder. "We'd never think of you as a thief, Miss."

"Ladies spend a lot on their trinkets, don't they?" Davy muttered, wide-eyed as he stared at the coins.

"They do," I agreed. "Especially the women who aren't quite high class, but want to be seen as such. They'll drop a fortune to appear fancier."

"Well, lass," O'Doule said, "Although some is in silver, it's the value of twenty gold pieces."

"Wow," McGee breathed. "There's more money in ladies' fancywork than rum-running. Who knew?"

I shook my head. "I hadn't added it up in some time. This is crazy."

Teeth, Davy and Larry all hurried to the bunk room to their private stashes. With O'Doule keeping count and making change, they traded in a few gold coins for the silver, until we had twenty gold pieces gleaming in the lamplight.

Slipping them back into the makeshift purse, I asked, "How does one go about bribing a guard?"

Everyone grew very serious. "In calm little towns like this, they usually put their worst guard on the late-night shift," Davy said. "It's often the man who's a bit..." He tapped his forehead with a grubby finger. "Slow. They only hired him because he's someone's cousin or the like."

"True," O'Doule said. "These small towns are always family first. Let's use that." His eyes darted around to the other men. "I'd rather use cunning than the pistols, lads. That's what the Captain would want."

They nodded in agreement.

"If he's been on the night shift a while, he might be jumpy all alone," Teeth said thoughtfully. "Maybe we give him some sort of scare?"

"Aye," McGee said. "What are slightly slow small town men afraid of?"

"Ghosts."

"Pirates."

"McGee's rotten attempt at meatloaf."

"Their own shadow."

"Women!" Davy laughed.

The men all howled with laughter, then Larry stared down at his hands, thinking. "He's right. Many of these young men haven't dealt with many women beyond family. A gorgeous lass strutting in and availing herself to his mercy would shake him to the core."

They all turned to me with questioning glances.

"They would never arrest a woman, would they?" I whispered.

"No, lass, never," O'Doule said quickly. "Not unless you'd murdered someone right in front of them. For a minor inconvenience, they'd turn you away and threaten to tell your father on you, at worst."

My hands were in fists, squeezing my skirt as I tried to think. "What sort of woman goes down to the jail to ask for a man to be released?" I asked.

McGee snapped his fingers. "His wife! You say that you're his poor little wife, and the Captain is a drunken lout, and you need to drag him home."

"Before his mother finds out what he's done this time," Teeth added. "Every man is a bit scared of his mother. We're also scared of other men's mothers."

The men all nodded. McGee looked at me very carefully. "Do you think you can act a bit hysterical, lass? Crying and yelling? No man could stand it if a sweet lass was pitching a fit."

"He'd do anything to comfort you," Larry agreed. "Miss Flora, this is a lot to ask. But if you were the one to go in, there would be no threat of violence. I'd be right outside."

"Me too," said Davy. "You say the word 'pumpkin' and we'll rush in and start breaking bones."

I shuddered, then felt Larry's heavy hand on my shoulder. "It won't come to that," he said gently. "Even the sharpest guard's defenses will fall apart at the sight of you being flustered. It's truly playing dirty, in a way, but it is pretty much guaranteed to work."

"Have you been working on your yelling, lass?" O'Doule asked. "Would be best to yell at the start, then cry. Shock him."

"Aye, put him off kilter," Teeth agreed.

Larry patted my shoulder again before pulling his hand away. "You just finished that lovely blue dress, didn't you? You'll look delicate as a fresh flower in it. Any man would be desperate to help you."

Looking around the table at five eager faces, I began to nod. They had all been so helpful to me. And the Captain himself had given me this new life full of more beautiful things than I ever could have imagined.

Standing up slowly, I tried to find my voice. "Davy, go watch the jail so that you can tell us when the night guard starts. I'll get dressed."

I'd never heard five boisterous men cheer for me before, and I was shocked at how much I enjoyed it. It felt good to have a team with me. They felt like brothers, of a sort.

***

Two hours later, I was shocked at how much I enjoyed this. Putting a plan together, working as a crew, and trying to be brave. It was more adventurous than I would have ever believed.

Davy had casually walked around the town until the jail's shift change, strolling back near the ship to signal O'Doule.

Then he meandered back to hide under the jailor's window to listen in.

Larry left the ship first, casually strolling down the dock to the shore. Although I'd never seen him smoke before, he lit a cigar, walking around as if he were simply enjoying the night air.

I waited for several minutes before leaving the ship, glancing around as if I were simply admiring the boats in the light of the nearly full moon. I almost panicked when a dockhand from a much smaller ship jumped down onto the boards near me.

"Begging your pardon, Miss," he said. Then he took a good look at me, and the ship I obviously came from.

He was a plain fellow, but he had kind eyes as he leaned in to say, "Miss, a proper lady such as yourself might not belong with those ruffians. If you need to get clear of them, there's a ship leaving for Glenbert at noon tomorrow. I've heard there are nice, sensible people there."

My smile couldn't be contained. I knew in my heart of hearts that I would never return there again. Whether the Captain owned me, or some other strange circumstance befell me, there was no way that I'd ever go to my old home.

"I appreciate your concern," I said as smoothly as possible, "But kindly mind your own." I raised an eyebrow, practicing a haughty glare.

To my surprise, he jumped back as if he'd been slapped. "So sorry, Miss, 'twas not my place." He disappeared into the shadows as I walked away with my head held high.

My home was on The Fortune's Favor, and I couldn't imagine being anywhere else. Still, it was rather nice knowing that my decision was completely final.

I followed the path down toward the jail, then as it grew more narrow, I slipped into the darkness beside a stable. Creeping in the shadows, tiptoeing down a smaller path so the townsfolk wouldn't see me, I felt like a thief. Like a scoundrel. I felt, dare I even think it, like a pirate.

~ Chapter 20 ~ The Captain ~

** Son of a… **

"Where the hell is my no-good drunk husband?"

The shriek from the front of the jail made me jump to my feet. Sitting in the near dark, I'd been thinking for hours of how to escape. The building was the sturdiest I'd ever seen, so it would take an act of great cunning.

Perhaps now that there was a hysterical woman for the guard to deal with, it might be my chance. I'd heard bits of conversation as the guards switched shifts. Clancy told Thomas that there was only one prisoner overnight, but that he should ignore me. He hadn't bothered saying why I was there, as he seemed in a rush to leave.

Thomas hadn't seen me yet. I wondered if there was any way I could finagle my way out.

"Where is he?" the woman yelled. Her loud, shrill voice echoed off the stone walls, creating an eerie vibration. She sounded like she was filled with rage.

"Hold up there, Ma'am," the guard said. I stared up the hallway, wishing I could see what was going on around the corner.

"No, you hold up," she snapped. This woman sounded angry enough to throw a punch. But then she made a sob that nearly broke my heart. "Please, sir," she wailed. "His mother is going to kill us both if I don't have him on time to church tomorrow morning. It's his niece's christening, and if he's not there, she'll think it's my fault again."

Son of a… Was that Flora?

My mind raced. I'd never heard the shy lass speak above a ladylike murmur. I must have been mistaken.

"Please," she cried dramatically, "I know he's a drunken lout, but he's never done anything truly terrible."

"You know I can't do that, ma'am."

"Just let me take him home to sleep it off," she loudly begged. I heard a jangling noise. "Perhaps this will help you make up your mind?"

"Holy mother of…" The guard gasped. I couldn't hear anything for a moment. "Er, I suppose accidents happen, Ma'am. I guess this will cover the trouble of me erasing his name from the record."

"That's so very kind of you. You're a darling man. Now please, I need to get him home as quick as I can to start scrubbing him up for the morning."

Hearing the guard coming down the hall, I quickly pulled my shirt collar askew, messed up my hair, and leaned clumsily against the wall. I had just enough time to yank at my bottom lashes so my eyes would appear glassy, an old trick my former Captain had taught me. Playing a drunkard was the easiest role for such a situation.

The guard dashed to the door, his hands shaking as he worked the key. Over his shoulder, I saw Flora looking positively radiant. She flashed me a brilliant grin and a wink, then her pretty little face clenched in a scowl.

"You rat bastard," she hissed. "You know what your mother will do to you if you're not in church tomorrow."

"Darlin'," I drawled drunkenly. "You asked the nice man to let me out?"

The second the guard had the door open, she grabbed my ear, leading me roughly down the hall, cussing me out the entire time. She'd obviously heard every single word that Davy and Teeth had used last week when they were repairing the rigging.

The guard wasn't able to get a word in as we passed the desk, where she stumbled for a second, then hauled me out the front door.

"You be quiet and not wake the neighbors," she said angrily as she led me up the path.

She released my ear, but didn't stop walking as quickly as possible. "Don't look back," she whispered. "Larry and Davy are right behind us, and the Fortune's ready to sail the second we're on deck."

The farther we were from the jail, the faster Flora moved, until she was practically running down the path with her skirts hitched up to her knees. I heard two men behind us, one with a quick light step, and one with a heavy thump. "Lads," I murmured, keeping pace with Flora as they came up right behind us.

"Cap'n," they both said quietly.

Flora was glorious. Her delicate face was slightly flushed from nearly running. Her tidy hair was now messed up and rippling behind her. The skirts of her pretty new dress were clenched in her fists as she hoisted them out of the way.

I loved this woman. I knew it already, but now it was even more clear. We were meant to be, sure as the stars.

The second The Fortune's Favor was in view, I saw the sails were already half raised, and only one rope held the ship steady. We raced along the dock and up the plank. As soon as the four of us were on deck, Teeth slipped the rope and we glided away. Once the sails were up and the ship was headed out of the channel, the crew all gathered on deck.

We stood in silence for a few minutes, waiting until we were safely away from the town.

Then O'Doule laughed. "By crikey, it worked!"

Tossing Flora into the air in joy, watching her flaxen hair float around her in the moonlight, I was dazzled by my sweet girl. Catching her in my arms, I gave her a swift kiss on the forehead. I knew it was inappropriate in front of the men, but I couldn't help it.

"Flora, lass, you were magnificent," I said, unabashedly filled with awe. I knew if I paused another heartbeat I wouldn't be able to keep myself from kissing her, so I hugged her to my side. "Lads, I think after that we all need a drink."

"Ale or rum, Captain?" McGee asked. I shot him a look. "Sorry. Rum it is."

~ Chapter 21 ~ Flora ~

Round Table with Rum

We settled around the table in the galley, each of the men with a mug of rum in his hand. McGee had given me a mug as well, with a splash of rum and a few splashes of water. I noticed that the Captain had pulled his barrel right next to mine.

I took a tentative sip, trying not to flinch at the odd sensation. It really did warm me straight through, then seemed to calm me down. My heart was still racing from our adventure.

"How did you get that much money?" the Captain asked with a wide grin. "Did you boys all pool your savings?"

"It was Miss Flora," O'Doule said warmly. "The clever girl had been saving every cent from her necklace sales. She didn't even know how much she had, since she'd never thought of spending it."

Looking over to the older man with pride sparkling in his eyes, I realized that this was how a father should speak about his daughter. Tears prickled as I blinked them away quickly.

O'Doule grinned. "Most of it was in gold, and we traded out the rest to make a tidy sum that no man could resist."

I was shocked when the Captain wrapped his arms around me in front of the men. "Little lass, I'm sorry you had to spend all of your money on me. I swear, I'll–"

He paused when he heard a sharp jangle. Reaching into the hidden pocket in my dress, I pulled out the tiny sack. "I might have, purely accidentally mind you, picked up my purse from the desk as we rushed out."

Six rugged, tanned faces stared at me, utterly shocked. Then Davy and Teeth burst into laughter, and the rest joined in.

"Well, Miss Flora," O'Doule said, "Not that there was ever any doubt that you were one of us, it's clear now."

The Captain kissed the top of my head, and I snuggled into his side. "I'm so proud of you, lass," he said. Turning to the men, he grinned. "You should have heard her. She sounded half-crazed."

Larry and Davy nodded. "Aye," Davy said. "I heard a bit through the window. Our Flora could act in the theater, she could."

"You were truly wild, Miss," Larry agreed. "I almost felt sorry for the guard."

"He'll recover," the Captain said. "His pride was hurt but not a scratch on him. Just a story to tell, to be sure."

"So," O'Doule said slowly, looking to the Captain, "This seems to be proof that smuggling and trading might be a tad safer for us lot than outright piratin'?"

The Captain didn't answer, simply looking around as the rest of the men nodded. I respected that he listened to the whole crew, his decisions depending on the opinion of the group.

"Aye." The Captain nodded thoughtfully. "We haven't run up the black in a long while, and I don't think we ever will again. Perhaps we should create a new flag. Something more respectable."

"With stars."

"With a fish."

"And a mug of rum."

"Gold pieces."

"Plaid."

"Ye can't have a plaid flag."

"Well, ye can't have a flag with a fish, ye daft–"

"*Boys!*"

Everyone turned in shock at my exclamation. I had raised

my voice to them. At first I was as shocked as they were, until they all grinned. It looked like each man was practically bursting with glee.

I took a breath, then continued more calmly. "First we ask the question, what message do we want to say with a new flag? It's how far off ships introduce themselves. What do we want strangers to think of us?"

I looked up at the Captain. "What does this ship represent above all else?"

"Traveling," he said. The group nodded in agreement.

"What do travelers need besides a good ship?" I asked.

"The north star," Larry said.

"The sea," O'Doule added.

I jumped up to grab a few sheets of paper and a pencil where I'd been trying to write down recipes to teach McGee. Flipping it to the back, I drew out a rectangle for the flag, with a star by the top right, and two wavy lines under it.

"The sea and the star," the Captain said thoughtfully. "Wishing on a star is lucky."

"Aye, that's how we have good fortune," Larry agreed. "The Fortune's Favor, the North star and the sea. That sums up our whole lives."

I felt the Captain's hand stroking the back of my hair, and turned to him. "And a flag designed by lucky number seven," he said proudly.

"That's just the first idea," I said quickly "We can all think on it for a spell."

"We're headed to Leclard Island soon," O'Doule said. "There's a shop there that sells sail fabric. They'd have material for a flag."

I sipped from my mug mostly to hide my little grin, but I was becoming more accustomed to the taste of this odd warming drink.

The Captain must have caught a whiff from my mug, as he grabbed it and took a sip. "You're drinking rum?"

"With water, Captain," McGee said quickly. "Just a drop for the wee lass."

For half a second, I wondered if he would be disappointed with me. But the Captain grinned widely. "Finish your drink, my lass, and let's get you to bed."

~ Chapter 22 ~ The Captain ~

** Purchase **

"That was a hell of a chance you took, lass," I said gently as we walked to our quarters. "The thought of you being caught by the guard… I just can't even think it."

"Larry and Davy were outside, you were inside, and there was just one guard. The men all said that there was no way anyone would hurt a crying woman."

I chuckled as I opened the door for her. "You yelled so loudly in that jail I didn't even realize it was you at first."

"Forgive me, sir, I know it's improper…"

I closed the door behind us, grabbing her around the waist as I kissed her swiftly. "Lass, I am so proud of your performance. I just wish you hadn't had to do it." I cupped her sweet face in my hand. "The thought of you in pain or discomfort rattles me, lass."

"It's sweet how you worry about me."

I looked at her in surprise. Then I ran my rough thumb along her soft cheek. "Of course, darling girl. I'll always worry about you."

"Always is a long time," she smiled gently.

I looked at her sharply. "What do you mean?"

"Oh, nothing, sir," she shook her head. "I just sometimes wonder… I mean, things seem to ebb and flow out here. Nobody ever mentions any time more than a few months out."

I felt stricken. "I would never… sweet girl, you must know that I need you forever?"

She bit her lip, staring down at her hands.

"Please," I said, taking her hand in mine. "Speak plainly, girl. What troubles you?"

Flora went to sit on the bed, patting the spot beside her, and I sat close. The wee thing looked so serious that it was making me nearly jumpy. She dug in the hidden pocket of her skirt, fishing out the purse of coins, and placing it in my hand.

"Lass, I have no need for your money."

"I'm paying you back for buying me." Flora looked up into my eyes with fierce determination. "Sir, I don't wish to be owned."

It felt like my blood was leaving my skin, everything growing cold. "Lass, you... you're not wishing to leave?"

"No!" she exclaimed, giving me a quick kiss that shared enough heat that I was reassured somewhat. "My life is here with you on the Fortune, and I've never been happier."

I set the money on my lap and held her hand. "What's all this then?"

"I'm yours because I want to be, not because I must. I want to be your girl, not your property. Er, if that's alright with you, sir."

Her smile was as soft and warm as a sunrise. "My sweet girl. Delicate as a rose petal, sharp as a needle, but tough as fine steel." I hefted the sack in my hand, then stood up and turned to the wall behind us. Sliding my thumb under a piece of wood, I popped out a hidden panel, stowing the sack within and replacing the plank.

Turning back to Flora, I sat close again, wrapping an arm around her. "Let's save that bit of gold and spend it together someday."

She grinned sweetly. "That's a fine idea."

"My lass, I never thought of you as an acquisition. I paid your father so that he wouldn't sell you to a scoundrel. The thought of what other men might've done to you... I just had to keep you safe."

"I swear, I've never felt like you had a hold on me. And I'm plenty grateful for all you've done. But if I'm going to be a woman of the world and the sea, I want to be my own woman as well as yours. Do you understand?"

"Yes, my love."

Flora's eyes grew huge. I realized I may not have used that word before. I'd hoped that I'd been showing her my feelings all along, but I was scarcely an expert with women. Perhaps they needed to hear things more clearly.

She reached up to stroke my brow, running her thumb around my eye, down my cheekbone, to my bottom lip. My tongue darted out to touch it, and she giggled.

"And now, as your equal and not your possession, I have a demand."

"Anything, my fine lass."

"Anything? You promise?" She looked up at me with more determination than I'd ever seen from her.

"Aye, ye have my best word."

Standing up, her fingers trembled as she unbuttoned the cuffs of her fine new dress and began to slide it off.

"I don't think I've told you how bewitching you look in that bright blue," I said gently. "When I first saw you in the jail, it took a moment for me to breathe."

The blush that washed over her cheeks caught my attention. Then she slipped the dress off, then her knickers, standing in front of me absolutely naked.

Flora was perfectly still, delicate at a flower at dawn. My eyes raked over her fair skin, her sweet womanly curves. Indeed, she'd changed a bit over the past few months. Her thighs were more shapely from running around the ship and the beaches. Her hips were curvier from solid meals. Her breasts were round and soft, and in my hands before I could think, pulling her against me.

"Lassie, I cannot believe what a fine woman you are. You truly take my breath away."

She was obviously enjoying my touch, as I caressed her skin, circling her nipples until they were delicious little points. I leaned in to suck one, the sound of her tiny gasp making me smile against her.

"Mmm, please… sir… I need to say something."

I sat up straight, placing my hands around her waist. "I'm listening."

"It's just that... well, sir..."

I could feel her shaking. "Lass, you can say anything to me. Take your time."

"You purchased me, but never used me for what I had assumed in the beginning I was intended for. Which is fine. Your ship, your rules. If you don't want me in that way, that's for you to decide. But I just can't help but wonder why you haven't taken me completely."

I interrupted by pulling her into a soft, wet kiss. My hands gently caressed her lower back, then shifted lower to cup her behind almost roughly. My lips traveled south, kissing down her chin, her throat, down to nip the top of her breast until she gave a tiny squeal.

"Lassie," I said, in a voice thick with lust, "Don't ye think for one moment that I don't want you the way you're thinking."

"What are you waiting for?" she whispered.

"I already have everything I want. You, my little treasure."

"You don't think I'm ready?" She seemed so determined. I loved how fiery the once timid lass was becoming.

I scooped her up, sitting her in my lap, still wandering my hands all over. "I suppose it's time for us to have a talk." She nodded nervously.

I reached out to tuck the loose strands of hair behind her ear. "My sweet girl. You're so tiny, so fragile. The thought of hurting you hurts me terribly, do you understand?"

She nodded. "Yes. You always take such good care of me. But why don't you want... that?"

I rocked her gently. "I do. Very much. But if we were to do that, it would hurt you."

"Why?"

"It always hurts the girl the first time." I sighed heavily, shaking my head. "Did your mother not explain this to you?"

"She said to let the man do what he needed to, and don't bother fighting," she shrugged.

"Hell's teeth," I muttered. Taking a deep breath, I thought

for a few moments before speaking. "Lassie, your lady parts have never been opened by a man. So things will be very tight. But you're so tiny, and I'm so big, that it would be, shall we say, uncomfortable for you. The first time will likely hurt."

She blushed brightly, but forced herself to continue. "I, um, have heard of the maidenhead. But wouldn't it get better after a few times?"

I shook my head sadly. "I don't know. And I don't know if that's a chance I'd want to take with you, little one."

"What if…" she hesitated, her cheeks turning nearly crimson, but I nodded for her to continue. "What if it's a chance that I want to take?" she asked. "You said that out here on the sea, there are no rules. If I want to do something, I should do it. Right?"

I was so proud of her for being brave, even when she was embarrassed. And even when she disagreed with me. I grinned, giving a little chuckle. "S'pose I did say that."

"Well, I want to try." Her eyes were determined, but I could see the twinge of nervousness deep within.

"Tell you what, lass, I'll think about it."

Her fingers began unbuttoning my shirt. Then I felt her soft hands on my chest. I wasn't sure why that always stirred my blood. Watching her be so bold was arousing in a way that I couldn't make sense of.

Standing up, I laid her on the bed, shucking my clothes to snuggle under the blankets with her.

"We've had a busy day, and you've likely had a fright. If we were responsible people, we'd go straight to sleep," I teased.

"Good thing we're actually pirates," she said, her eyes flashing in the dim light. She grabbed my face with both hands and kissed me so hard my heart raced in my chest. Flora pressed her forehead to mine. "I demand that you take me."

I'd never wanted a woman this desperately in my life. I'd never needed anything as much as I needed to plunge inside her. For her to give me an order like this was the most arousing thing a man could ever hear.

***

~ Chapter 23 ~ Flora ~

** Please **

I'd never demanded anything in my entire life. Since he was the Captain, I knew that he could laugh it off if he really wanted to. But I needed him to feel how serious I was.

Having him laying over me felt so right, as my legs spread, pulling him against me. His arousal was hard as steel, nudging against my skin. I felt so open, so ready. I needed to feel him completely. I'd been craving him for weeks now. It was time.

We kissed with such fire that it felt like he lost himself for a moment, his hand gripping my hip as he began to press against me. Then he stopped.

"I can't hurt you lass. I just can't. After seeing how every man in your life has brought you pain, I cannot do it." He looked at me in absolute anguish.

I felt my lips press together as I thought intently for a second. "What if you weren't the one to do it?"

He eyed me suspiciously. "What on earth do you mean?"

"Well, what if... um," I blushed, wishing once again that the Captain would just ravish me completely instead of this awkwardness.

"What if I were the one doing all of the moving, so that it was completely my fault if anything hurt for a moment?" I suddenly blurted.

"Hmm," the Captain contemplated. "I've always said that you're a clever lass." He rolled us so that I was on top of him.

Instantly I felt my juices flowing as my hips moved of

their own accord. Sliding myself along his length, I saw his eyes blaze.

Reaching down, I stroked his thick shaft, loving the feeling of his body trembling from my touch. The tingling charge between us was nearly too much.

My body took over, as my desire told me exactly what to do. Straddling his hips with my knees wide, I rubbed his tip around my opening. Watching his eyes locked on to where we were about to join sent a thrill up my spine. His hands gripped my behind tightly as his gaze wandered from my breasts to my open thighs.

Leaning slightly forward, I pressed the head into my flesh, rocking, wiggling as he began to slip inside.

"Gently, sweetheart," he murmured, a worried but keen look in his eyes. "We have all night. Go slowly."

Having him watch me as I pushed my body onto his length was savagely erotic. My hands fanned across his chest as I rocked my hips, moving down a tiny bit more.

His eyes fell closed for a second, and I couldn't believe how close I felt to him at this moment. Then I tried to work him deeper, but didn't have the strength. Or the angle. I was afraid of bending him in a painful direction.

Taking a slow breath, I moved his shaft in and out again, then quickly tried to drive deeper. I felt tears of frustration brewing, blinking them quickly away.

"See, lassie? I'm sorry, but I'm too big for you."

I gripped his face between my palms, staring into those mysteriously dark eyes. "I need you on top of me, now. I need you to try for me, now."

His grin met my lips as he kissed me, his hands stroking my skin with such a soft touch. He rolled me onto my back, lying beside me. Still kissing me deeply, his hand slid down my stomach, between my legs.

The feeling of his finger inside me made my entire body feel warm, as if I were melting beneath him. Then he slowly thrust two fingers all the way in and out of my passage until I felt like I was dripping wet.

I reached down to stroke him. I could feel the change in his kiss the second my hand wrapped around his flesh, smoothly running up and down his length.

A gasp overtook me as a third finger stretched me. It was a little too much, but it felt too good. Like desserts that were honestly a bit too sweet but one could never stop eating them.

Our hands both moved faster, and I could finally feel a shift deep within him. As the Captain settled over me, still kissing me, I felt a wave of sultry calm overtake me.

He dragged the head of his member through my crease over and over, until I was quivering, nearly whimpering.

"Please," I begged shamelessly. "Captain, I need you."

A low growl from the back of his throat told me how much he needed me as well. I felt his shoulders tighten under my hands as he began pressing inside me slowly.

"Mmm, yes," I moaned. The feeling of him filling me was so perfect. He slid as deeply as he could without applying any pressure, then stopped, taking tiny, gentle strokes.

"Please, sir, I..."

He stopped, pulling out immediately. "Did I hurt you?"

"No. I need..."

"Anything, darling."

Every part of me was filled with the most urgent desire. My eyes were wide with desperation. "I need you to treat me like a possession now. Please... take me... I beg you."

I wrapped my legs around his hips like a strong vine. Finally the Captain could not restrain himself any longer. "Lassic, ye must tell me if it hurts too much."

"You could never hurt me, Captain," I murmured into his ear. Grasping his shoulders, he began to truly plunge inside my snug, eager passage.

He was indeed too big for me, but I was so wanting, so ready, so wet that he began to ease inside. Pressing my lips firmly together, I was carefully silent as he thrust through my innocence, possessing me completely. Swallowing my gasps, I clamped my eyes tightly shut so they couldn't tear up.

The pressure was overwhelming, my small body confused

at the intrusion, but my primal instincts took over and soon I felt nothing but fire and lust. The more I relaxed, the more the pleasure took over.

"Oh, yes..." I sighed, as my body opened for his. His massive shaft was spreading my tunnel walls, molding me to his body. My feelings surged as my energy did. I'd never known that devotion could be expressed with anything but words and sweet kisses. This feeling of physical love was a force greater than the sea, as we rocked together slowly.

The Captain scooped an arm under my shoulders, holding me against his chest as he burrowed deeper. A low moan escaped his lips. "My lassie, you feel like heaven on earth." He was desperately trying to be gentle, but it felt like it was hard to control his passion. He had sunk well over half of his thick rod inside me, and seemed worried to go further.

"That feels incredible," I murmured, lunging for his lips, kissing him wildly. Our tongues entwined as our bodies did, sultry and wet, drawing pleasure with and for each other.

He leaned back to study my face in the glow of the lamplight. "Does it hurt, my angel?"

I grinned up at him wickedly. "Not anymore, my Captain. Please... fill me more."

Cautiously he nudged deeper, as he ran his lips along the hollow of my throat. "So snug, so soft, my wee lass. My lovely precious girl."

I squeezed my legs against his backside to propel him lower, further into my depths. "Oh... yes..." I moaned, working my hips against him in a wave. Too many feelings and thoughts were flooding me at once, and my whole body was twitching from bliss.

As our skin became one flesh, I was astounded at how close, how intimate this act was. He could hear my every breath, every moan, practically every thought as I lay naked under him. Yet instead of being vulnerable, I felt powerful from the way his broad shoulders stirred when I wriggled him deeper, as I opened for him. This great man, the strong and dominating Captain of the Fortune, was shuddering in my arms, flushed and wanting.

As he rocked inside me, always stroking further, I felt the burning pull in my core, as if flames were waiting to be released. His lips meandered along my breast, closing around my nipple to suck gently. I clutched his head as I began to quiver.

"Kiss me as I..." I begged. As his mouth settled over mine, my center exploded in a crashing of warmth, all tension released as I moaned beneath him. My tight little tunnel flowed with juices, and he was able to press even deeper.

"Oh, lassie," he groaned, with a tender ferocity. His hips moved faster, propelling him with a force that surprised and delighted me. The feeling of him completely consuming me was positively divine.

"Yes," I squealed, overcome by both sensation and emotion. "Yes, Captain!"

He kissed me savagely as he thrust deeper, and his low grunts drove me mad with passion. "Take me, Captain," I gasped, "Harder... please..."

His powerful body quivered, then I suddenly felt his entire frame shudder as bursts of his hot liquid erupted inside me. My urgent cries were muffled by his lips, as I instinctively tightened inside, passionately caressing him to the end.

"Oh, my love..." he growled, searching my eyes as the last tremors rattled through him. "I love you, Flora. My sweet girl."

"I love you, Captain."

He rolled to the side, clutching me against him snugly. Then I felt his chuckle under my cheek, sitting up slightly to study his dark eyes. They were softer. Like the gentle breeze after a storm had passed.

"Do you remember when you grabbed my collar, offering to fix it on the day we met?"

"Yes."

"Do you have any idea how hard it was not to kiss you right then?"

I giggled. "We'd barely met."

"Which is why I didn't." He leaned up on his elbow, his other hand meandering along my shoulder, through my hair. "The funny thing is, back then you would have been so terrified, you would have let me. But now, you would have slapped me quite properly."

I nodded. "That's likely true."

His grin caused the few wee lines around his eyes to crinkle adorably. "I think I'd prefer an honest slap to a terrified kiss. I'm glad you've found your voice, little lass."

The Captain leaned in to kiss me, then I slapped him gently, barely brushing my hand on his cheek. "What's that slap for?"

"For not kissing me harder," I said, raising an eyebrow haughtily.

Pulling me close, he kissed me until my toes curled, my hips quivered, and my fingers dug roughly into his shoulders.

"Hard enough?" he finally breathed.

"Keep practicing."

"Arr," he growled, "You saucy little…"

~ Chapter 24 ~ The Captain ~

* *New World* *

Although I drifted off for a spell, I bolted awake again. Perhaps I was just too joyous to sleep.

Ever since I'd made the decision to rename the ship, fortune had been in my favor. Except for the one bit of unpleasantness in Parrinport, and the fact that we would have to find new towns for Flora to sell her jewelry, our new life of shipping and trading was going brilliantly.

Having Flora on the ship had brought balance to our crew. She lightened the mood. There was more joking and laughter, and the joviality was in slightly better taste much of the time since a lady was present.

The food was much better, which improved everyone's mood overall. We had new clothing, which always made the men feel well cared for. The raggedy sails were being repaired steadily.

We were becoming respectable. This sat well with the older crew members, as they weren't risking their lives and health with every voyage. The younger boys seemed to prefer it as well. They wanted to work hard, not fight hard. Yet they also wanted to relax on a beach now and then. Our new trade route was providing us this luxury, and this would increase as time went on.

My view of the future had always been a bit murky, as I took things from day to day. Flora was right. Time was different out here, and tended to ebb and flow with the tides.

Hearing the gentle swish of the waves against the hull,

I looked out the window. I'd once sworn that I'd never stop living on the sea. But I knew that someday I'd end up living right beside the sea, and there was only one woman who could understand the difference properly.

Flora had been more than patient while learning to live an entirely new life, in an entirely new world. The very least that I could do would be to make one tiny thing stable and permanent.

~ Chapter 25 ~ Flora ~

* *Under the Moon* *

"Lass, wake up for a moment."

"Hrm?" I blinked hard, trying to focus. Not so long ago, a man's voice in the night would be terrifying. Now I simply reached out to snuggle against the Captain's chest, feeling warm and safe.

The Captain sat up, pulling me with him, so we were facing the tiny portal that looked out over the sea. The full moon was clearing the horizon, sending feathers of silver across the water.

He waited while I stared at the sea for a moment, then cleared his throat. "Lass, I thought of the perfect way we could spend that extra gold together."

I looked up at him with a smile, curious and excited. "What's that, sir?" He had an odd look about him, and although I'd never seen him wear the expression before, he looked nervous. Taking my hand, he looked at me quite seriously.

"We'll be down in Port Chancelry in a week. What do you think about getting married in the south?"

I froze, my mouth falling open. I couldn't move for three full heartbeats while the Captain held his breath. "Are you..." I cocked my head, blinking, terrified I might be misunderstanding.

"I love you, Flora. You're the most magical creature on land or sea, and I'd be honored to have you as my wife."

My breath hitched with a tiny choked cry as I held back a

sob. Throwing myself into his arms, he rocked me softly. "Yes. I love you, Captain," I whispered. "Yes, that's a beautiful idea, to be wed in the south."

He wanted to marry me. No dowry, no connections. Just me. He wanted to keep me as his. Just a few months ago, I would have fallen to pieces at the thought. Now, it made me feel strong. Secure. As if every part of my world clicked into the proper place.

This wonderful man thought I was valuable enough to bond me to him forever.

The Captain pulled back to study my eyes carefully. "Unless you want to return to your village for the ceremony. If you want your mother to be there, or your girlfriends. I know that brides like a maid of honor and such."

"I don't need any of that. I never want to go back there." The moment I said it, I knew once again that my decision was absolute.

"We could have Little Larry wear a dress," he teased.

"I already have a fine, strong woman who can stand up for me," I grinned. Reaching out, I patted the wooden wall. "The Fortune's Favor will be there, right?"

"Aye, that's my clever lass," he said. We dissolved into a kiss, snuggling down into the bed again, wrapped in each other's bodies while our ship gently sailed with the evening winds.

~ Epilogue ~ Flora ~

Flora's Paradise / Cabbages

"Mama, what's the name of our island today?"

I grinned, reaching out to rumple little Artie's thick curls. He had his father's dark eyes, but I thought it would take him some time to grow into his father's name. Arthur didn't quite fit for a six-year-old. Maybe when he turned sixteen.

"Did you ask your sister?"

His pudgy face scrunched up in a scowl, just like his father's did when a storm was rolling in. But holding his little hands in fists when he was frustrated definitely came from me.

"Clara always says the island is called Sandy Land." He glared at me as if I should have known better.

I laughed, turning him to point down the beach. "Do you see where Uncle McGee is making us a new storage cabin? Maybe he knows what the island is called today."

"Okay," he chirped. His little feet took off down the pale sand.

Looking around our island paradise, a tiny dot on the horizon caught my eye. Hearing footsteps behind me, I stepped back into the arms that circled around me. "Yes, that's the Fortune," the Captain said before I could even ask. "Davy and O'Doule will be here in time for supper."

Since our crew now had friends in every port to assist with loading, the ship could make trading runs with just two or three crew members.

Looking down to the west end of the beach, I saw a heavy plume of smoke coming up from the shack where Teeth was working with his new forge. We had dropped him at his Uncle Rupert's for a few months, to learn the ways of silversmithing. He'd always been a hard worker, but now that he was doing something he truly loved, it was hard to even drag him away for meals.

Artie ran past us toward the forge hut, yelling, "Uncle McGee has no idea so I'm going to go ask Uncle Teeth."

"Let him know when you're close, and don't go inside," I hollered across the soft ocean breeze.

The Captain's thick arms gave me a squeeze. "Look at you, hollering like a very improper lady," he chuckled. "Don't worry, the lad knows better than to cross the lines Teeth set out for him."

We'd purchased a forge, and all of the supplies and tools so that Teeth could learn the trade. Now he and I designed jewelry together, while I still made accessories from shells and ribbons as well.

The Fortune's Favor now delivered dry goods, spices, and materials to twenty-five different ports on a monthly schedule. It was easy to sell anything we liked.

"Why don't I make us a big family supper tonight?" I asked the Captain. "That way Anna won't have to cook." Since Larry's wife was expecting her second child within the month, I was trying to make things easier on her.

"Always so clever, this lass of mine," he said, rocking me against him. "I'll go tell Larry, then I'll come back to help."

Spinning quickly, I surprised him with a kiss. At first I simply meant to be saucy, but then I felt the way his hand gripped my behind roughly, pulling me firmly against him.

"You best not be thinking about a third baby," I tried to growl.

He stuck out his bottom lip in a childish pout.

"But we can practice all you like," I giggled.

The Captain's handsome grin nearly took my breath away, as it always did. Stepping back, he took my hand, kissing the back of it, then kissing the lovely golden ring we had found together in a tiny shop in Aberbryn.

"M'lady," he bowed. Then he hurried off to Larry and Anna's cabin.

The six little houses spread out at the edge of the forest just beyond the sand made our own tiny village. Now that we had a silversmith hut and would soon have three storage sheds, plus a giant outdoor dining canopy, we were creating our own small town.

That's why none of us could agree on a name for the island. It was growing so fast that we didn't want to put a label on it, for fear it would be wrong in a few years. So for now, we changed the name every few days, or whenever the wind shifted.

I looked over to where Clara and Lizzie were running strange little races in the sand. They made some kind of line with rocks on one side and sticks on the other. There seemed to be a complicated pattern of the two of them running back and forth.

Lizzie was just two months older than Clara's three and a half years, and they were practically sisters. Larry and Anna were expecting again. A very cleaned up Davy was now courting a nice girl in Chancelry. I wondered how large the population of the island would grow.

Artie came running up to me with a huge smile on his wee face. "Uncle Teeth says that the island is called Cabbages today. So, the cabbage is sacred. We're not allowed to have them for supper."

I knelt down to give him a hug. "Okay then, we're going to need lettuce and carrots." I held up my hands a foot apart. "Can you be my little farmer and pick that much lettuce for us?"

"Okay."

"And six big carrots. How many is six?"

He held up one hand and one finger, rolling his eyes. "I can count to fifty now, you know."

I stood up and grabbed the gathering basket from a hook by the door, handing it down to him. "I know. I was just checking."

"Okay, Mama," he smiled, scampering off to our giant garden patch.

The Captain returned, grabbing me and spinning me into a hug until I giggled in his arms. "Larry caught a pheasant this morning, so he'll clean it up and roast it in the fire pit for dinner."

"Artie is fetching carrots and lettuce."

"I thought the cabbages were ready?"

I looked at him very seriously. "Aye, but since that's the island's name today, it cannot be eaten."

The Captain shrugged, all too accustomed to this nonsense. Then his hand cupped my face, his thumb running along my cheekbone with such tenderness it turned my insides to pudding. "You know the island is really called Flora's Paradise," he whispered softly.

He had told me this a thousand times, but I needed to hear at least a thousand more.

"I don't know why I keep forgetting that," I murmured, stretching up to kiss my incredible husband.

He'd taken a girl who believed she was worthless, and transformed me into the queen of my own island. I'd never had any dreams of my own until the day he bought me. And now every single one of them had come true, yet there was still room for plenty more.

*** *The End* ***

LATEST NOVEL:

Whispered Curses – Tea time prophesies, accidental insta-love, and dealing with one's demons.

Eden:
Nana once told me, "Never get in bed with the devil."
I assumed she meant to stay away from bad men.
If anyone got hurt because I didn't listen to The Knowing, I'd never, ever forgive myself.
After a tipsy encounter with a guy who was hotter than Hades itself, I thought I'd found the one.
Finding out his real name was like a bucket of cold water on the flames of my fascination.
The thing that scared me the most? My Nana's never been wrong before.

Eric:
I'd never been a superstitious person.
But after what Eden told me, I could understand why she was afraid.
I did everything in my power to help her trust me.
The fire between us was too powerful to be denied.
Yet if I pushed too hard, I might become the evil man she'd been warned about.

COMING SOON:

Heart Shaped Spotlight
It's one thing to pine for the perfect man you lost years ago. It's another thing to turn on the TV and hear him singing directly to you.

NOVELS:

Love in the Darkness: A shy girl alpha male romance novel

A week in the dark has them seeing everything in a new light.

Kayla: Accepting help from anyone makes my skin crawl.
With my eyes bandaged for a week, I have no choice.
When a huge tough guy shows up instead of my usual nurse, I
don't know how to act. But he cares for me so sweetly, I could
learn to get used to it. Every time he touches me, I feel utterly
cherished. Treasured. He's strong, thoughtful, and achingly
seductive. I can't wait to see his face. To hopefully be his
girlfriend instead of his patient.
Liam: Although I can't see her eyes, I fall for Kayla's lovely
soul. Her clever, delicate way of viewing the world. (So to
speak.) I'd do anything to keep her safe and healthy. And even
more to touch her silky skin. Kiss those perfect lips. Even
though I know once she looks at me, she'll want to run. All I
can do is care for her as long and as much as she'll let me.

Donuts and Handcuffs: A sweet, floury, mixed-up love story.

A budding baker. A caring cop.
A sweet and spicy romance of opposites.

Daniel: When this sweet girl literally tumbled into my life, so
did my heart. I want nothing more than to protect her from the
haunted shadows in her beautiful eyes. Yet clearly she isn't
ready to share her past. To trust me. My uniform should be
enough for her to know I'm a good guy.
Bailey: I could see myself with Daniel. But he's a cop.
And I have too many things to keep hidden. Besides, I'm
busy running a new bakery, starting a new life. No time for
daydreams of the way he touches me, the way he truly listens.
Being with me could ruin his reputation, a risk I couldn't take.
No matter that he melts me like butter across hot bread.

The Librarian and the Rock Star
They say that opposites attract – especially when people are searching for change at the moment they meet. It's a catalyst for a fascinating week and a half.

Marry Me, Right Now
When a rich man needs a fake wife and a broke woman needs a home fast, a marriage of convenience goes faster and farther than they expected.

NOVELLAS:

Like short romance novellas? Up Love - Insta Love Shy Girl Romance" Series. *(Just 99¢ / free with Kindle Unlimited)*

#1 - Icing up Love – When a cake decorator meets a former hockey player, the icing meets the ice in a whirlwind romance.

#2 - Packing Up Love – When a moving man falls for a damsel in distress, his overprotective urges are too heavy for a girl labeled, "Fragile".

#3 - Snapping Up Love – Will an event photographer keep his focus when the perfect model steps into his life?

#4 - Inking Up Love – Can a tattoo artist keep his hands steady when the girl of his dreams walks in the door?

#5 - Snipping Up Love – When a billionaire visits a new hair stylist, 'a little off the top' becomes 'over the top'.

#6 - Roasting Up Love – A cafe owner brews more than java when he meets a web designer with an empty mug and an empty heart.

#7 - Serving Up Love – A billionaire hands a sweet event server his own heart on a silver platter.

#8 - Fixing Up Love – When a shopkeeper's life needs a tune up, her local mechanic finds a way to wrench open her heart.

About the Author

Romance author Haley Travis is from Toronto, Ontario, Canada. She enjoys writing quirky, sexy modern romance, and loves creating interesting female characters who are at a turning point in their lives. Women who need a life shake up, not a man. But these things never go as planned, do they?

Do people ever read author bios? Maybe this is a good place for secrets. Like the Facebook group "Haley Travis Romance".

***

Want to be a hero to an author you enjoy?
Review their work online.
Even if it's a super short review, it really helps increase visibility. On most sites you can change your name to initials if you'd like to maintain your privacy.

Thanks for being one of the cool people
who still read books!